'The romance of the island is finding its way into your heart. It happens to everyone after a while. It casts a spell on you, and you never want to leave.'

Ethan came to stand in front of her, laying a hand on the bole of the palm tree just above her head, and then he leaned towards her, dropping a kiss lightly on her mouth.

'I hadn't expected it to happen,' he said softly, 'but you've made a huge impact on my life. You caught me unawares, and now I can't stop thinking about you—day or night.'

He made a half-smile, his gaze running over her. 'Especially in the night.'

He kissed her again, teasing the softness of her lips with the brush of his mouth, enticing a flurry of expectation within her nervous system, stoking the flame that burned inside her.

When **Joanna Neil** discovered Mills & Boon®, her lifelong addiction to reading crystallised into an exciting new career writing Medical™ Romance. Her characters are probably the outcome of her varied lifestyle, which includes working as a clerk, typist, nurse and infant teacher. She enjoys dressmaking and cooking at her Leicestershire home. Her family includes a husband, son and daughter, an exuberant yellow Labrador and two slightly crazed cockatiels. She currently works with a team of tutors at her local education centre to provide creative writing workshops for people interested in exploring their own writing ambitions.

Recent titles by the same author:

NEW SURGEON AT ASHVALE A&E
POSH DOC, SOCIETY WEDDING
HOT-SHOT DOC, CHRISTMAS BRIDE
THE REBEL AND THE BABY DOCTOR

HAWAIIAN SUNSET, DREAM PROPOSAL

BY
JOANNA NEIL

First published in Great Britain 2010
Large Print edition 2010
Harlequin Mills & Boon Limited,
Eton House, 18-24 Paradise Road,
Richmond, Surrey TW9 1SR

© Joanna Neil 2010

ISBN: 978 0 263 21129 0

Harlequin Mills & Boon policy is to use papers that are
natural, renewable and recyclable products and made
from wood grown in sustainable forests. The logging and
manufacturing process conform to the legal environmental
regulations of the country of origin.

Printed and bound in Great Britain
by CPI Antony Rowe, Chippenham, Wiltshire

31652204

HAWAIIAN SUNSET, DREAM PROPOSAL

CHAPTER ONE

'HE'S not doing very well at all, is he?' The young woman's voice was choked with emotion, and her eyes filled with tears as she looked at Amber. 'Isn't there something more that you can do for him? Nothing seems to be happening.'

Amber removed the printed trace from her patient's heart monitor and taped the paper strip into his file. The readings were erratic, showing a dangerous, uncoordinated rhythm. 'I know this must be a very difficult time for you,' she said in a quiet voice, turning towards the girl, 'but I want you to know that we're doing everything we can for your father. I've given him an injection to take away the pain, and he's receiving medication through a drip in his arm to try to prevent things from getting any worse.' There was a defibrillator on standby in case his condition deteriorated, but she wasn't going to point that out to her patient's anxious daughter.

The girl pulled in a shaky breath. 'He looks so dreadfully ill. I know he hasn't been well these last few months, but this has come as such a shock. As soon as I saw him, I knew it was bad. His secretary called me at the university to say that he was unwell and that they'd called for an ambulance… I was in the middle of a lecture, and I rushed over there as quickly as I could.'

She gulped, sending a worried glance towards her father. 'She said he had been in his office, trying to get through a backlog of work, when he suddenly felt nauseous and short of breath. At first he thought he was suffering from a bad attack of indigestion, but then things got worse and he felt this awful pain in his chest…a crushing, vice-like pain.'

She broke off and dabbed at her eyes with a tissue. 'By the time I arrived at the office, he had collapsed and the paramedics were there. It all seemed to have happened so quickly.'

'The paramedics gave him emergency treatment before they brought him here,' Amber told her. 'They did everything that was possible to make sure he arrived here safely.'

Martyn Wyndham Brookes had been conscious when he'd arrived at A and E but, despite his pain and discomfort, his one thought had been for his daughter. 'She's very young,' he had managed to say, 'and she's a long way from home…studying at university. She always wanted to come to London.' His face had been haggard with pain, but his concern for his daughter had been obvious as he'd looked anxiously at Amber, and she had hurried to reassure him.

'We'll look after her, I promise,' she'd told him gently. 'I'll have a nurse take care of her…but right now we need to concentrate on making you feel better.' She had taken to him straight away…such a strong, warm-hearted man.

Now, after he had lapsed into a drowsy, semi-conscious state, she felt it was time to explain to his daughter what had happened. 'I suspect he's had a heart attack,' she said, 'and that there's a blood clot blocking an artery somewhere and causing problems with his circulation.'

Tears trickled down Caitlin Wyndham Brookes's cheeks. 'That's what the paramedic said…but that's bad, isn't it?'

'It's something we're used to dealing with,' Amber said. She studied the girl's pale features. 'Is there anyone we can call for you…someone who might come and be with you?'

Caitlin shook her head. 'My mother died some years ago, and there's no one over here…just my friends at university.' She gazed at Amber in an agitated fashion. 'Isn't there something more you can do for him? What if you have to go off and deal with other patients? I know you have others to see, and it's so busy here. There are so many patients being brought in… I want somebody to be with him all the time, someone in a senior position.'

The flow of words stopped suddenly, as though she was taking stock of what she had said. 'It's not that I'm doubting your ability,' Caitlin tried to explain, 'but he's just lying there, looking so frail… It isn't like him at all…he's always been so tough, so busy, on the move all the time.' Distress caused her voice to waver, and Amber hurried to soothe her once more.

'We'll know much more about what's happened to him when we've done all the necessary tests. It will take a little while for all the results to come back, though. In the meantime, we're taking good care of him. He's receiving oxygen through a face-mask, and his condition is being observed the whole time with the aid of the heart monitor and various other machines. If I'm called away to attend to another patient, I'll still know what's going on, because the nurses will alert me to any change as soon as it happens.'

She frowned as she ran the stethoscope over her patient's chest. Initially, his heart rate had been alarmingly fast, while his pulse had been barely discernible, but now the heart rhythm was becoming chaotic and everything about the man told her that he was gravely ill.

'Unfortunately, we don't have any records for him, over here in the U.K.,' Amber said, turning to look at the girl once more. Caitlin Wyndham Brookes was twenty or so years old, a slender young woman with black hair expertly cut into a smooth, jaw-length bob. Her eyes were grey, sombre at the moment, much like an overcast, rain-drenched sky. 'You mentioned that he lives overseas for most of the year,' Amber added. 'Do you know who looks after his medical care back home?'

'He has his own doctor in Oahu…in Hawaii.' Caitlin glanced at Amber. 'I suppose I could try to get in touch with my step-cousin over there. He'll be very concerned about my father— they're so much like father and son. My father took Ethan under his wing after his parents died, and there's a real bond between them.'

She hesitated for a moment, thinking things through. 'Ethan would probably be able to have a word with the doctor back home, if that would help, and I know he'll want to be kept informed about what's happening over here.'

Amber nodded. 'That would be great. As he's so far away, it might be quicker and easier if he could fax the information we need, or perhaps send the bare essentials by e-mail. If you were to go and have a word with our nurse, I'm sure she could help sort things out.'

Sarah, the nurse on duty, was happy to oblige, and Amber sent her a grateful glance as she led the young woman away. Sarah gave her a discreet smile in return, her fair hair making a silky swathe across her shoulders as she nodded with gentle perception. 'I'll take a few details and see if we can find out any more information.'

She could see that Amber had enough on her hands, dealing with a difficult situation that could take a turn for the worse at any moment. Much as she wanted to help in any way she could, Amber was finding it distracting, trying to keep the young woman calm throughout everything.

Amber turned her attention back to her patient. Martyn Wyndham Brookes was in his mid-fifties, a tall, personable man, she guessed from talking to the paramedics, with black hair streaked with threads of silver. She gathered that he was a wealthy man, a man of some standing in the international business community. According to the paramedics who had brought him into hospital, his U.K. office was situated in Docklands, occupying a prestigious block that overlooked the grand vista of the river Thames.

It seemed, though, that illness was no respecter of wealth or position. Martyn's condition had gone downhill rapidly, and Amber knew that it was going to take all her skill to help him to recover. His features were ashen, his skin had taken on a clammy appearance, and he was no longer attempting to talk.

'How's it going?'

She glanced up to see that James, her boyfriend, a senior house officer like herself, had come to join her. She looked at him with affection, feeling as though a faint glow of sunshine had come into her life. 'Things could be better,' she said in a low tone. 'It's always good to see you, though. How are things with you?'

He shrugged, draping an arm around her shoulders, so that she immediately felt warm and cherished. 'So-so. It's been pretty stressful around here, lately, with one thing and another. We're still waiting on the results of job applications, aren't we, and our contracts here come to an end within a couple of weeks? Have you heard anything yet?'

She shook her head. 'Nothing, so far, though I haven't had time to check my hospital mail box yet today. We've been so rushed in here.'

He gave a brief, half-hearted smile. 'I expect you'll come through it all right. You're very good at everything you do. Look at the way you sailed through your exams. No one is going to turn you down. You applied for a top-notch job in emergency medicine and you're bound to get it.' Even as he was singing her praises, there was a flat note in James's voice that made Amber glance up at him, a frown indenting her brow.

He let his arm fall to his side, leaving her feeling suddenly bereft. Something was clearly wrong with him, but she had no idea what it might be. James had not been his usual self for some weeks now. At first she had thought it was the pressure of exams weighing him down, along with the aftermath of results, but now she was beginning to wonder if it was something more than that.

'I don't think it's as cut and dried as it seems. I'm waiting to hear the news just the same as everyone else. From what I've heard, it's all down to the computer system matching up job applications with employers. There were some terrible glitches, apparently.' She frowned. 'It's all a bit worrying, isn't it? Sarah said that there have been quite a few mix-ups, and a lot of people have missed out on getting any kind of job. Some junior doctors have been talking about leaving medicine altogether.' She shook her head in sad reflection, causing her burnished chestnut curls to quiver in response. 'It's such a waste, after all those years of training.'

She looked back at her patient. He seemed to be oblivious to everything that was going on around him, but perhaps that was just as well, given how desperately ill he was.

'I doubt you'll have any problems,' James said.

'All the senior staff speak very highly of you, and you could pretty much do anything you want. I guess it puts me in the shade.' His mouth made a rueful shape, and Amber sent him another quick look, wondering what had got into him to make him appear so downbeat.

'You sound as though things are becoming too much for you,' she murmured, sending him a sympathetic smile before checking the pulse oximeter reading to see how her patient was doing. The machine kept bleeping, warning her that the level of oxygen in his blood was falling as his circulation became more impaired. She decided to check with the consultant about starting him on thrombolytic drugs to try to dissolve, or reduce, the size of any clot that might have formed.

'I'm really hoping that we'll be able to work together at the London University Hospital. We've worked well with one another here in A and E, haven't we?' Amber studied James closely, seeing the troubled look in his eyes. 'Perhaps we could have lunch together later today and talk things through? I'm fairly sure that you won't have any trouble getting the research job you were after.'

'Maybe. There aren't that many people lining up to study my particular area of enquiry into asthma. It all depends whether the powers that be can come up with the funding.'

He straightened up, looking more at ease with himself, and moved away from her, towards the door. 'I'll go and check in the office again to see if any more news has come in.' He looked at the man lying motionless in the bed. 'Poor chap. It looks as though he's having a rough time.'

Amber nodded, brushing a hand over her temples to tease back tendrils of hair that threatened to obscure her vision. Her chestnut-coloured hair was a shoulder-length mass of wild curls, a genetic gift from her mother that needed to be ruthlessly tamed with clips or scrunches. They shared the same eye colour, too, a soft, jewelled green.

'I want to start him on thrombolytics,' she said, 'but until I have the results from the lab, I'm working in the dark a bit. My boss is operating on a badly injured patient right now, and I don't want to disturb him unnecessarily, but I don't think I can afford to wait.'

'I know what you mean. It's a balancing act, knowing when to prescribe and when to bide your time. I'd be inclined to interrupt your boss if I were you.' James walked towards the door. 'I'll be back down here in a few minutes to see how you're doing—I only came to see if you had heard anything about the job you applied for. Someone said letters were being given out this morning but for now I need to go and check up on a patient. Do you want me to check your box for any letters while I'm there?'

'Yes, thanks.' Amber nodded and turned her attention back to the businessman, writing up his medication notes on the chart as Sarah came into the room. Sarah shot a glance towards James as they passed each other in the corridor, and a small frown started up on her brow. Martyn's daughter was by her side, but Caitlin was preoccupied just then, speaking to someone on her mobile phone. She stayed in the doorway, and Amber guessed Sarah had asked her not to bring the phone into the room.

Amber put the chart to one side and looked once more at the chest X-ray in the light box. Martyn's heart was enlarged, and that was not a good sign.

Sarah inspected the settings on the infusion meter and made sure that their patient was receiving the right amount of medication through a drip in his arm.

'Is everything okay with you and James?' she asked in a quiet voice, throwing a brief glance in Amber's direction. 'He doesn't seem to be his usual self these days, does he? It's hard to pinpoint, but there's definitely something…'

'I was just thinking the same thing,' Amber answered cautiously. 'I think the world of him, as you know. We've been together for over a year now, and I thought everything was fine, but just lately I'm not so sure. He doesn't smile as often as he did, and he has a sort of hangdog air about him, doesn't he?'

Sarah nodded. 'It's probably the aftermath of

exams, and waiting around for results and job offers,' she remarked. 'It seems to have affected everyone. My boyfriend's gone into a bit of a decline, too. We've just not been having any fun lately.'

'I dare say things will get better.' Amber looked across the room at Caitlin, and saw that there was an awkward air about her, a reticence, as though she was in some way holding back. 'Was there something you wanted to ask?' Amber murmured.

Caitlin indicated the phone. 'It's my step-cousin, Ethan,' she said, in a hesitant fashion. 'He asked me to put him on speaker-phone. He wants to be involved in everything that's going on.'

'That's fine with me.' Amber nodded. 'Just don't bring the phone any closer to the medical equipment, or it might cause interference.'

She checked Martyn's pulse. It was thready, his features were drained of colour, and she was worried in general about his condition. 'It must be frustrating for your cousin to be so far away and not know what's happening.'

'But not for much longer, I hope.' A male voice

cracked in a whip-like fashion across the room. His tone was concise and authoritative, and Amber braced herself in startled recognition of the fact that he must be able to hear every word that was being spoken. 'I'd like to talk to the doctor in charge of my uncle's case,' he said.

'That would be me,' she answered. 'I'm Dr Amber Shaw. I'm the senior house officer in A and E. I was on duty when your uncle was brought in. I take it you are Ethan Wyndham Brookes?'

'I'm Ethan Brookes without the Wyndham. Yes, my cousin explained the situation to me. I understand you've been taking care of my uncle, and I'm grateful to you for that. I heard that you have him on anti-coagulant therapy to prevent any more blood clots from forming, but his condition seems to be deteriorating.'

'Things are going very much as we might have expected,' Amber told him. 'As I explained to your cousin, we're still waiting on the results of tests, but they should be here very soon.'

'Hmm. But in these situations time is of the essence, isn't it? So, I'd like to speak to the consultant in charge, if I may?'

He posed it as a polite question, but Amber was in no doubt that it was a request. She guessed from his deep, well-modulated and assured tones that he was used to having things his own way. He would be somewhere in his mid-thirties, she imagined.

'Of course, I'll put you in touch with him as soon as possible, but he's in Theatre at the moment. Perhaps I could assist you in the meantime? I'd like to reassure you that we're doing all that we can to make your uncle comfortable.'

'I'm glad to hear it. My cousin and I are very worried about her father.'

Amber had the feeling he didn't want to be dealing with an underling at all, but she made an effort to remain calm and not take it personally.

'I'm very well aware that this is a difficult time for both of you,' Amber murmured, 'but I can assure you that everything that can be done is being done. Your uncle has received the recommended treatment so far...oxygen, aspirin, glyceryl trinitrate and painkilling medication, as well as blood-thinning drugs. I've already cleared the way for him to be taken up to the angiography suite. As soon as my boss has finished in surgery, he'll come down and assess your uncle's state of health.'

'So you're thinking about operating on him?'

'It's a possibility, if his condition will allow us to do so. We may be able to find the clot that's causing the damage and remove it by means of a catheter. That might do away with the need for more intrusive, major surgery, but I have to say that Mr Wyndham Brookes's condition is very precarious. From the looks of his X-ray there could be an underlying disease that might cause more problems. That's why it would be extremely helpful for us to have access to his medical records.'

'I'm already onto it, and I'll send them to you as soon as possible. In the meantime, I'd like to set up a video link with his hospital room. I know you have conferencing capabilities, so it shouldn't be too difficult to arrange.'

His suggestion took Amber's breath away. This

man clearly knew what he wanted, and didn't see why he shouldn't sweep every obstacle to one side in order to get things done.

'Is that going to be a problem for you? Perhaps I should speak with your chief administrator?' Perhaps he had heard her swift intake of breath. Ethan Brookes sounded as though he had no time for shilly-shallying. If she couldn't deal with it, he would go to someone who could.

'That won't be necessary,' she murmured. 'Your uncle is in a private room, so I'm sure we can accommodate your request, as long as his daughter has no objection.' She glanced at Caitlin, raising her brow in a faint query.

'I'd like that,' Caitlin said. 'It will make me feel better to know that Ethan's looking on.'

Amber wasn't at all sure how she felt about it. Having her every move watched by a stranger wasn't something she welcomed, but technological advances meant that it could be done, and if it was something that helped unite families in their hour of need, who was she to object?

'My boss should be here within a few

minutes,' Amber said. 'I'll speak to him about it, and if he agrees, we'll call on one of our technicians to set it up. Now, if you don't mind, I need to give my full attention to your uncle…unless there was something else that you urgently wanted to discuss?'

'No…it will keep. Thanks for your co-operation,' Ethan said. The speaker-phone link was cut, and Caitlin went out into the corridor to finish her conversation with him in private.

Amber drew in a deep breath. It was one thing to deal with worried relatives close at hand, but having difficult, long-distance discussions with someone she had never met was a first for her.

A few minutes later, she left Martyn in Sarah's care, while another nurse took Caitlin away to show her to a waiting room. There she would be able to sit in comfort and talk about her concerns to the nurse with the aid of a reviving cup of tea. Having Caitlin looked after took a great deal of the strain off Amber's shoulders and left her free to go and check on her other patients.

When her boss came down from Theatre,

Amber grabbed the opportunity to update him on Martyn's condition.

'We'll take him up to the catheter suite as soon as the team is assembled,' the consultant agreed. 'As to the video link, I see no reason to object.' He gave a brief, wry smile. 'Besides, I've heard of the Brookes's international fruit-shipping company. I read about their goings-on in the newspaper from time to time. These people are high-powered, influential individuals. Let's not get on the wrong side of any of them, if we can help it. Call the technician and ask him to sort out the video link. Anything to keep them happy.'

Amber lifted a faintly arched brow. Her boss wasn't someone who usually worried too much about following protocol and treading carefully around people, so if he thought it expedient to appease Ethan Brookes, who was she to argue?

'Professor Halloran,' Sarah interrupted, 'you're needed in the resuscitation room. One of your pacemaker patients is in difficulty.'

The consultant nodded. 'Okay, I'll be along right away.' He sent a brief glance towards

Amber. 'Prepare Mr Wyndham Brookes for surgery, and I'll be along as soon as possible.'

Amber did as he asked, leaving a nurse to call in the technician to set up the video link. Martyn was barely conscious, but she spoke to him gently, explaining what they were going to do.

'Professor Halloran is the best cardiac surgeon we have,' she told him. 'He'll use X-ray images to look at your blood vessels through our cardiac monitor, and that should help him to find exactly where the blockage is. He'll most likely insert a very thin catheter into a blood vessel of the top of your leg, and then he'll use specialised instruments to remove the clot that's causing the problem.' She looked into his grey eyes. 'Do you understand what I'm saying?'

He nodded almost imperceptibly. 'I do.'

'Is there anything that you'd like to ask me about it?'

'Nothing. Thank you. I'm very tired.' He tried to lift his hand and made a frail attempt to pat hers as it rested gently on the bedclothes beside him. His breath came in quick gasps. 'I know you'll do your best for me. You mustn't worry if it all goes wrong.'

Amber felt the quick sting of tears behind her eyelids. Somehow, this man had managed to reach her inner core, the place where she tried to keep her feelings hidden. In the short time she had known him, she had found an affinity with him, and she realised that she cared deeply about what happened to him.

'Nothing will go wrong,' she said softly. 'I'm going to take good care of you, I promise, and you have to know that Professor Halloran is the very best.'

He didn't speak any more after that, but lapsed into what seemed like an exhausted sleep. The heart monitor began to bleep, the trace showing a chaotic descent into a dangerous rhythm, and Amber called for help. 'I need a crash team here— now. Call for Professor Halloran.' Her patient was going into shock, and cardiac arrest was imminent. 'He's in V-fib.' Ventricular fibrillation meant the heart was unable to pump blood around Martyn's body and without swift intervention he would die.

James and Sarah rushed to the bedside. Sarah started chest compressions, while James set the defibrillator to analyse the patient's rhythm and prepared to deliver a shock to Martyn's heart. Amber was aware of Caitlin standing in the room, watching everything that was going on, tears rolling down her cheeks, but she couldn't let that distract her. She worked quickly to secure Martyn's airway with an endotracheal tube and ensure that he was receiving adequate oxygen through a mechanical ventilator.

'Stand clear, everyone,' James said. As soon as the shock had been delivered, Sarah continued compressions. Amber checked for a pulse and looked to see if the rhythm of the heart had changed.

'He's still in V-fib,' she said. 'Let's go again with a second shock.' By now, Caitlin was making small sobbing sounds, and Amber was aware of another strange background noise, an odd swishing sound that she couldn't quite make out.

James set the machine to deliver the second jolt

of electricity, but Amber could see it hadn't had the desired effect. 'Keep up the compressions,' she said. 'I'm going to give him a shot of adrenaline.'

They continued to work on their patient, but after a while, when Martyn's response was still insufficient, Amber added amiodarone to his intravenous line. She wasn't going to give up on this man, no matter how resistant his condition seemed to her efforts.

'You can do this, Martyn,' she said, under her breath. 'Come on, now, work with me. You're going to the catheter suite and you're going to come through this. Don't let me down.'

James glanced towards Caitlin, clearly disturbed by the girl's distress, but he could see that Sarah was tiring and moved to take over the chest compressions. Sarah watched the monitors and recorded the readings on a chart, while Amber worriedly assessed the nature of the heart rhythm and debated whether to add atropine to the medications she had already given him.

Professor Halloran came into the room, taking everything in with one sweeping glance. 'How's he doing?' he asked. 'Do you have a normal rhythm now?'

Amber checked the monitor and turned towards him. 'We do,' she said, relief sounding in her voice, and Professor Halloran nodded in satisfaction.

'Well done, everyone.' He turned his attention to the flat screen of the computer monitor that had been set up on a table across the room. He held up his hands in a thumbs-up sign. 'He's back with us,' he addressed the screen, and now, at last, Amber realised where the swishing sound had been coming from.

The screen was filled with the image of a man standing on what appeared to be a wooden veranda, surrounded on all sides by a balustrade. He was looking towards them, long limbed, lean and fit, with broad shoulders that tapered to a slim, flat-stomached midriff. He was wearing casual clothes made of fine-textured cotton that would be cool and comfortable in the heat of the Hawaiian summer. In the background she made out a palm tree and the clear blue of ocean waves lapping on a golden, sandy beach.

'I see that,' the man said. 'I saw it all, as clearly as if I had been there.' He moved closer to the webcam, and Amber realised that the computer must be situated on a ledge in front of him. The screen showed him now in clear view, blotting out most of the background, and she was aware of the strong, angular lines of his face, of thick, black hair cut in a way that perfectly framed his features. Most of all, she was stunned by his clear, blue eyes, the exact colour of the sea, that appeared to be looking right at her.

'We'll take your uncle up to the catheter suite right away,' Professor Halloran said. 'It's important that we get to work as soon as possible.' He glanced at Amber. 'I'll leave you to bring him up in the lift, Amber, while I go and prepare.'

Amber nodded, dragging her gaze away from the image on the screen. She was glad to have something to distract her. There was something about the way Ethan Brookes looked at her that was infinitely disturbing. It was as though he could see into her very soul, and that was an unnerving thought.

Even more unsettling, though, as her gaze swivelled to the doorway, was the sight of James, deep in conversation with Caitlin.

'I don't know what to do,' Caitlin was saying. 'He's all I have in the world.'

'You're not alone,' James murmured. 'I'll look after you. I'm off duty for a while now, and we can talk. Maybe we could even get together later this evening when my shift finishes. I know you'll probably want to talk some more. These things can hit you very hard. It's a worrying time.'

The girl lifted tear-drenched eyes towards the young doctor, and James reacted in the way that men have reacted throughout time. He melted in the face of her vulnerability, draped an arm around her and gently led her away. It was an innocent, caring gesture, but somehow, seeing his tenderness and concern for this young woman, it rocked Amber to the core. James hadn't taken his eyes off Caitlin's face. He looked at her with compassion and something else, something akin to adoration. He appeared to be totally, utterly smitten.

'Dr Shaw? Are you with us?' Ethan Brookes's voice cracked across the void, and Amber blinked, coming back to reality and trying unsuccessfully to blank out the image that was imprinted on her mind.

'I should thank you for your prompt action,' he said, and she lifted her gaze towards the screen once more.

Those steely blue eyes raked over her, as though he was making a thorough assessment of her. 'You've bought my uncle a little more time, and I'm grateful to you for that.'

She gave a brief, noncommittal nod in his direction. 'That's what I'm here for,' she murmured.

'Yes, but it's obvious that you're also young and relatively inexperienced. You did well to cope as you did…but I'm wondering if I should arrange for a private specialist to come and take charge of my uncle's case. I don't want anything left to chance.'

She braced her shoulders. She was a senior house officer, more than capable of doing what was required. 'Of course, that's your prerogative,' she murmured. 'It wouldn't be wise to delay proceedings, though. He needs to go to surgery now, and we have his full permission to go ahead…so if you'll excuse me, I need to go and take him there.'

'I understand that. I won't get in your way… now…and thanks again for what you did.'

Ethan Brookes was thanking her, but his words had an empty ring about them. The image of his cousin and her boyfriend came into her mind once more, and right now she couldn't help momentarily wishing that the Brookes family had never come into her life.

CHAPTER TWO

'WE'VE done all that we can for him for the moment,' Professor Halloran told Amber as they left the catheterisation suite some time later. 'We may have cleared up the immediate problem, but Mr Wyndham Brookes is still a very sick man.'

Amber nodded. 'At least you managed to remove the blood clot that was causing the trouble. It's unfortunate that he has a lot of other things to contend with alongside that.' Martyn was lucky to be alive, but from the results of tests and the indications they had discovered during the operation, his quality of life was going to be severely restricted.

'I expect his nephew will want to know exactly what we've found,' Professor Halloran added, 'although the medical notes he sent us were a good pointer to the cause of the problem.' He frowned. 'Ethan Brookes is certainly keen on being kept fully involved, even though he's living thousands of miles away. Maybe you could explain to him that his uncle will need to take great care with his health over the next few months.'

'Are you not going to talk to him yourself?' Amber looked at her boss in surprise.

'Yes, I will…later. Right now, I have to go back to my pacemaker patient. His needs are greater right now.' He gave her a beaming smile. 'Besides, I've every confidence in you. Talk to Miss Wyndham Brookes, as well. I'll speak to both of them this afternoon, when I'm free.'

Amber was glad he had such faith in her to do the right thing, though she suspected it was a ploy…he was a much better surgeon than he was at talking to patients. As to speaking to Martyn's nephew herself, she was conscious that Ethan wasn't entirely pleased that she was the one taking day-to-day responsibility for his uncle. He wanted the best…but Professor Halloran was not readily available to be there for him one hundred per cent of the time.

She went back down to A and E and went in search of Martyn's daughter. She could understand how distressing this situation was for the girl, but the image of James consoling her and leading her away with his arm draped protectively around her had been running through her mind over and over again as if in a film loop these last few hours.

Perhaps she was taking things too personally, though. Wasn't it entirely natural for any normal, thinking person to want to comfort someone in their hour of need? James was a good, kind man. She ought to be pleased that he was so considerate towards others.

While she had been in the catheter suite, James had apparently been working his way steadily through the mounting list of patients who had arrived at A and E. He met her as she walked over to the central desk in the unit a few minutes later.

'I picked up this letter for you from your mail box,' he said, handing her an envelope. 'It looks official, so it could be news of the job you applied for.'

'Oh, thanks.' Amber frowned, looking at the logo on the envelope. He was right…the letter probably contained the information she was waiting for. She glanced up at him. 'Did you hear anything about the job you were after?'

His mouth made a downward turn. 'Yes. It turns out I didn't get the job. The letter was waiting for me when I went back to the mailroom. They appointed another candidate, but wished me luck for next time.'

Amber felt an immediate rush of sympathy for him. 'Oh, James,' she said, reaching out to give him a hug, 'I'm so sorry. I know how much you wanted that post. You must be feeling really down about it.'

He nodded briefly, trailing an arm around her in return. 'I was almost expecting to be turned down, but it came as a shock, all the same.'

'It must have done. What will you do now?'

He gave a negligent shrug. 'I'll have to think about some of the other research projects available. They weren't nearly as appealing as this one, but at least I stand some chance of getting one of them.'

'Sorry to interrupt, Amber,' Sarah said as she approached the desk, 'but Mr Wyndham Brookes has just been brought back down to his room. His daughter is feeling anxious because he doesn't look too good…and I think she's been looking at the medical notes that were sent over from Hawaii—that was never going to make her feel better. Her cousin advised her against it, and so did Professor Halloran, but she was determined to go ahead anyway. Do you want to come and have a word with her?'

'Yes, of course. I'll come along right away.'

Amber sent a worried look in James's direction, but he was already lifting up a patient's chart from the tray on the desk, and she started to turn, getting ready to walk away with Sarah.

James frowned. 'I feel sorry for the girl. It's bad enough that her father has been taken seriously ill, but she's a long way from home and virtually on her own.'

'I expect she appreciated you trying to help her,' Amber murmured. She slipped the envelope into her pocket. If it was bad news about the job she'd applied for, she'd rather deal with it when she was on her own back in her rented apartment. 'You were very kind to her. I imagine she'll look to you for help from now on. I heard you telling her that you would be free to talk to her after your shift finishes.'

'That's right. Do you mind very much?' James asked softly. 'I know we said that you and I would have dinner together later on today, but she's not coping very well, and I don't like to leave her without support. Maybe we could all get together to eat. She might appreciate having a woman around.'

'I'm not so sure about that.' Amber's expression was subdued. 'I don't think I'm her favourite person at the moment. She was quite distraught, and I had the distinct impression she thought I wasn't doing enough to help her father. It happens, doesn't it, when people are ill and the situation isn't improving?' She had the feeling that Caitlin had passed that view on to her cousin, but to his credit he hadn't made any comment on that—to Amber, at least.

She sent James a thoughtful glance. 'But you go ahead and meet up with her if that's what you want to do. I have a thousand things to catch up with back at the apartment.'

It might have been her imagination, but she thought she detected a look of relief passing over James's face. Was he finding it too much of a strain lately, being the second half of a couple? Over the last few weeks she had noticed subtle changes in his manner towards her, though she had tried to tell herself it wasn't happening. Now it cut her to the quick to have to take on board the changes in him. She didn't want to believe that their relationship was falling apart, but all the signs were beginning to point in that direction.

'I might do that, if you really don't mind? I said I would help her as much as I could.' He made a fleeting smile. 'It's strange, but it appears we have a lot in common. It turns out Caitlin's studying pharmaceutical sciences and wants to go into clinical research, much the same as me. It's an odd world, isn't it?'

Amber nodded. So they were on first-name terms already, were they? Her gaze was bemused as she watched him walk away. She set off with Sarah towards the patient's private room.

'I don't think I would have had the confidence to give him the go-ahead to meet up with another woman,' Sarah commented in a low voice as they walked along the corridor. 'Seems like a risky proposition to me.'

Amber gave a shuddery sigh. 'I've a feeling you could be right, but without trust, what is there? If I tried to stop him, it would make me appear selfish and uncaring, and for his part he'd probably end up feeling thwarted and resentful.'

'You're too good for this world,' Sarah commented dryly. 'In fact, you have a lot in common with Martyn Wyndham Brookes, now I come to think of it. I feel really sorry for him. He seems like such a lovely man. Even though he was very ill when he first came to us, he managed to thank us for what we were doing for him. He was appreciative to all the nurses. He's one in a million… I suppose it must have been great for his daughter to have him come over to the U.K. to work for a few months while she's studying here.'

'I should imagine so. I take it for granted that my parents are fairly close at hand, though we don't see each other as often as I would like. It must be a bit lonely for Martyn's daughter, being so far from home.' Amber was making an effort to put all thoughts of James and her patient's daughter out of her mind. It was all supposition up to now, and she could be wrenching her heart unnecessarily.

'A great experience, though, coming to study at one of the best universities around. And she has a dishy cousin keeping in touch with her.' Sarah grinned. 'Now, that does make me envious…except I wouldn't want to be related to him. He's much more like eligible-bachelor material.'

Amber gave a rueful grin. 'Are you sure he's eligible?'

'Oh, yes. Professor Halloran told me so. The

family's rich, and he's always in the papers because some flighty madam wants to get her hooks into him.'

Amber gave a dismissive laugh. 'I don't believe that for a minute. I have a feeling that he's way too grounded to allow anyone to take advantage unless he wants it. Just talking to him puts my defences on alert.'

'That's because you're ultra-cautious—and you're much more of a touchy-feely kind of person. Talking to him via a screen and a microphone isn't the same as meeting up with someone face to face. Technology just doesn't do it for you, does it?'

'You should have been a psychologist,' Amber remarked with a faint smile. 'Is he online right now, do you know?'

'Yes, he is,' Sarah murmured. Her mouth relaxed into a soft smile. 'He spoke to me to ask how things were going in the catheterisation suite. I'd have given anything to stay and chat with him,' she added in an undertone, 'but his cousin beat me to it, coming into the room and wanting to tell him what she'd heard.' She rolled her eyes heavenward. 'He has everything, doesn't he? Good looks, energy and a fabulous office practically on the beach.'

'Perhaps he works from home,' Amber suggested. 'If his family owns an international fruit-shipping company, it could be that they live on site. Imagine being at work and watching the waves roll onto the beach while you cool down with a glass of something iced and delicious, made by your own company.'

Sarah chuckled. 'I doubt I'd get very much work done in those circumstances,' she murmured.

When Amber walked into Martyn's room a moment later, she saw straight away that he was in a state of exhaustion. Of course, he was still drowsy from the anaesthetic, but the readings from the various monitors showed her that he was very weak and that his heart was struggling. She checked his medication, adjusting the infusion meter, before turning to his daughter, who was sitting, waiting anxiously by his bedside.

The computer monitor with the video link was

set up so that Ethan Brookes would be able to see both his uncle and his cousin. Amber did her best to ignore the webcam while she spoke to Caitlin. She was aware of Ethan's image in the background, though, his features alert, his gaze watchful, and though she nodded towards him briefly out of politeness, she preferred to set about dealing with the flesh-and-blood person who was in the room with her.

'Professor Halloran asked me to let you know that he removed the blockage in your father's artery,' she told Caitlin. 'His circulation improved right away, and he should soon start to feel much better. Even so, it looks as though there has been extensive damage to his heart, and I'm sorry to say that I don't believe he will ever regain perfect health. It's important that you know that.'

Caitlin's gaze was cool and remote. 'Wouldn't he have stood a better chance if he had been operated on earlier?'

It was a faint barb, but Amber deflected it easily enough, knowing that the young woman was deeply upset and trying to come to terms with her father's illness.

'No, I'm afraid he wouldn't,' she said gently. 'Your father was already struggling with a heart that had been weakened by an infection of some kind. It must have occurred a while ago, and unfortunately it means his heart muscle is unable to pump at normal strength. The body tries to compensate for this, and as a result fluid builds up in the lungs, liver and legs.'

'What treatment are you planning on giving him?' Ethan Brookes's deep voice cut into their conversation. 'There are things that you can do to help him have a better quality of life, aren't there?'

'Yes, we can certainly do that.' Amber turned to look at the computer screen. Ethan Brookes's blue eyes seemed to pierce her like lasers, as though he would accept no prevarication. 'We'll give him medication that will enhance the capacity of the heart muscle. Professor Halloran has prescribed a cardiac stimulant. What we want to do is make the heart's pumping more effective, and at the same time reduce congestion.'

She turned back to Caitlin. 'I know this is going to be hard for you to accept,' she said softly, 'but your father is never going to be the man he once was. He's very frail and once he's up and about again he'll find that he's short of breath if he tries to do too much. He'll have to take things slowly and that means he will need a long convalescence.'

Caitlin looked bewildered. 'He's never going to tolerate that. He's always been so vigorous. The business has been everything to him, and I can't see him sitting back and taking a passive role.'

'I don't believe he'll have any choice,' Amber said in a quiet voice. 'He can look forward to a reasonable quality of life if he takes things easy. Perhaps you can help by encouraging him to do that?'

Caitlin looked at the computer screen, sending her cousin a look of complete bewilderment. 'The business is everything to him,' she said. 'How is he going to be able to hand over the reins?'

Ethan's reply was brisk. 'I'm his partner,' he remarked in a matter-of-fact tone. 'I'll have to step in and make decisions for him.'

'But you've never been involved one hundred per cent in the business,' Caitlin protested. 'How is that going to work? You know what he's like. He'll never sit back and allow others to take over.'

'You'll have to leave it to me to sort things out,' Ethan said. 'I'm more worried about how you're going to manage. You still have a few weeks to go at university before you have to come home, don't you? Do you want me to come over and help you out?'

Caitlin shook her head. 'No, I couldn't ask that of you. I know how busy you are, and you'll have even more on your plate now that this has happened. You can't afford to take time off from your work. I'll manage. Don't worry about me. I have friends who will help me to get through this, and it's comforting to have this link set up so that I'm able to talk to you this way. It helps to put my mind at rest knowing that you're at the other end of a phone.'

Amber looked at her with renewed respect. Maybe she was growing up fast because of what had happened to her father. She wondered what it was that kept Ethan Brookes so busy, if he wasn't taking an active role in his uncle's business. What kind of work was he involved in?

'Will you keep me informed of what's going on over there, Dr Shaw?' His voice cut into her thoughts, and she blinked, looking up at the screen.

'Of course. I shall take a personal interest in your uncle's welfare. It may be that once he's up and about, we can refer him to our rehabilitation unit. They're very good at helping people to get back on their feet and helping them to learn how to cope with their limitations.' She studied him briefly. 'I understand how difficult this must be for everyone to take on board, but if you have any worries or questions, you only have to ask and I'll do my best to explain things.'

Ethan nodded. 'I know it can't be easy for you, relaying everything to me from such a long distance, but I do appreciate what you have been doing up to now. I should warn you, though, that illness and frailty won't keep my uncle down for long. Even though it seems that he might be easy to manage at the moment, once he's sitting up and taking notice you're likely to find him quite a different kettle of fish.'

'I'll try to bear that in mind,' Amber said. She wondered why he was warning her. Did he not think her capable of dealing with a difficult patient? She doubted Martyn would ever cause her a problem…he seemed to be a likeable man, through and through.

She glanced towards Caitlin. The girl was talking softly to her father, lightly stroking his hand in a gesture of affection, and Amber decided that for the moment she was calm enough and probably had as much information as she could handle. It would probably be best to leave her to come to terms with her father's condition at her own pace.

She looked back at the flat-panel computer screen, taking in the breathtaking sight of the Hawaiian seashore in the background. 'Every time I see you, you're close by the beach,' she murmured, focussing once more on Ethan. 'I had assumed that you were talking to us from your workplace—perhaps I was wrong about that? I must admit I've been envying your lifestyle.'

He gave her a fleeting smile that lit up his features. 'I should have explained,' he said. He waved a hand at the villa behind him. 'This is where I live. I've been trying to call the hospital from here whenever possible. You perhaps don't realise that it's actually very early in the morning over here, not long past sunrise, and I haven't even had breakfast yet, let alone set off for work. Besides, if I were to ring from the office, my uncle would soon become agitated. He likes to keep his finger on the pulse of what's going on, and any sign of his workplace would be enough to bring his blood pressure up.'

'You're right… I hadn't even thought about the time difference. It's late afternoon here.' So late, in fact, that she was due to finish her shift shortly. 'Anyway, from what I can see of it,' Amber murmured, 'you have a beautiful home.'

'Thank you. I certainly appreciate it,' Ethan said. 'Maybe at a time when neither of us is quite so busy, I'll show you around the inside, via the webcam.'

'I think I'd like that,' Amber agreed. 'It won't

be quite the same as being there, but I'm sure to get something of the feel of the place.' Maybe technology wasn't so bad after all. She smiled. 'All that sand and sea and palm trees waving in the light breeze make me long for my summer vacation. Not that I'd ever be likely to go as far as Hawaii.'

Perhaps it was the smile that caused it, but Ethan's eyes widened a fraction as he looked at her intently. After a moment or two his gaze moved slowly over her, as though he was seeing her properly for the first time, and she was suddenly conscious of the clothes she was wearing—a skirt that fell smoothly over the curve of her hips to drape softly around her legs, and a snugly fitting cotton top. What did he make of her? she wondered. Did he only see her as young and inexperienced, incapable of taking proper care of his uncle?

'I'm sure you would love it here,' he said. 'I'll be sure to show you the landscape all around when you check in again.'

At that moment, Martyn made a faint groaning

sound, and Amber turned immediately to look at him. She moved closer to the bedside. 'How are you feeling?' she asked.

'A bit sore,' Martyn answered. 'And very tired… It's as if all my energy has drained away.'

'That's to be expected,' Amber told him. 'It's nature's way of telling you to take things easy.'

'That's not what I'm used to,' he said with a wry smile. His gaze wandered to the computer screen. 'I thought I heard voices,' he murmured. 'Ethan, my boy, I'm glad you're there. What's happening at the plantation?' He paused to drag in a shaky breath. 'Are you managing to keep on top of things?'

Amber raised her eyes heavenward. Caitlin and Ethan had been right when they'd said he wouldn't let go. Here he was, slowly coming round from the effects of an injection that had made him woozy and tranquil, and he was already asking questions. 'I'll leave you in the care of the nurse while I go and look in on my other patients,' she told him. 'Have a chat with your family, but don't go tiring yourself. You need to rest.'

She gazed at the screen and sent Ethan a look that spoke volumes. He nodded, and gave her a smile in return. 'I'll make sure of it,' he said.

Amber took her leave of Caitlin, and went to check on the rest of her patients in A and E. Before too long it was time for her to go off duty and make her way home.

Once she was back in her apartment, the reality of everyday life began to creep in, and weariness swept over her as she recognised that she was totally, utterly alone. She had no doubt that James would have finished his shift and be comforting Caitlin right now, and that left a bitter taste in her mouth.

She reached into her pocket and drew out the letter James had given her. She had been busy these last few hours, but it had taken all her reserves of willpower to keep herself from opening it until now. All her hopes for the future lay within the contents of this envelope, but James hadn't even asked her what it contained. Perhaps he assumed all would be well…or maybe his priorities had changed, now that Caitlin needed his support.

She tore open the envelope. 'Dear Dr Shaw,' the letter began, 'I am sorry to inform you that, due to a filing error, your application was mislaid, and unfortunately the position you applied for has been filled in the meantime. Please accept our deepest apologies for the mix-up.'

Amber scrunched the letter into a ball and pulled in a shuddery breath. All her dreams were gone in the blink of an eye. She was devastated.

She had worked hard throughout her training to become a doctor, and her one ambition was to specialise in accident and emergency medicine. Now that opportunity had been denied her, and she was to all intents and purposes going to be out of work within a few weeks. It was too late to pursue any other job offer because all the specialist applications were closed.

She wandered around the apartment, seeing nothing, struggling to take in the news. There was no point in ringing James to confide in him, and seek to find consolation together. If he had cared enough, he would have phoned her by now to ask how she was getting on, and she could only guess that he probably had other things on his mind.

Instead, she rang her mother. She, at least, would want to know the result of all her efforts, and Amber had already found a voice message on her answering machine asking her to get in touch.

'Oh, Amber,' her mother said, 'I never dreamed that they would turn you down... Well, they haven't, have they? It's all down to administration errors. Is there anything you can do now? Will there be other jobs you can apply for?'

'I doubt it,' Amber said in a resigned tone. 'It's too late now to sort anything out. All the specialist positions that would have interested me will have been filled by now. The most I can hope for is that I can apply for a locum post. I might be able to fill in when people are sick. It means going from one hospital to another, where I'm needed, perhaps, or working for short stints on contract—a few months at a time, maybe.'

'It might not be so bad as you imagine,' her mother commented. 'Perhaps something will turn up.'

'Let's hope so,' Amber murmured.

They chatted for a little while, about her mother's work as a graphic artist, and Amber enquired after her father, who worked as a general practitioner at the local health centre.

'He's out on call, at the moment,' her mother said. 'There seems to be a spate of people going down with flu. I think he's overworked and stressed just now—one of the doctors is off sick, and another is away on leave, so the practice is under a bit of a strain. He's had to take on a good share of his workload, as well as his own. We're both under a good deal of pressure at the moment and things are a bit tense between us at times. I have deadlines to meet, and nothing quite goes the way I want it. I told him what we both need is a good holiday.'

Amber could see how that prospect would be tempting. She could do with a break herself. She had a picture in her mind of boats tethered on a gently sloping beach, while waves lapped desultorily at the shore, leaving white ribbons of foam to fringe the golden sand. Exotic birds would fly from one palm tree to another…and there, in the forefront, gazing at the vista before him, stood a tall, bronzed figure, his blue eyes half-closed against the glare of the sun.

She pulled herself together with a jolt, frowning as she said goodbye to her mother. Why on earth would an image of Ethan Brookes come into her mind that way? Didn't she have enough problems to deal with, without him popping into her mind every other minute?

CHAPTER THREE

'YOUR temperature's way too high, Jack,' Amber told her patient, 'so I'm going to give you something to try to bring it down, along with medication to stop you from being sick.'

'Thanks. I feel really rough.'

'I can imagine how bad it must be.' She glanced at his arm. 'That's a really nasty sore you have there,' she said with a frown as she examined him. 'Do you recall how it happened?'

Jack grimaced. 'I was bitten by an insect of some kind—a sandfly, I think.' He was a man in his early twenties, a man who should have been full of vigour and zest for life, but at this moment his skin was sallow, and there were beads of sweat breaking out on his brow.

Amber nodded. 'I don't suppose that it happened in this country, did it? Have you been overseas at all, lately?'

'I was in South America,' Jack said. 'I worked there for a couple of months until recently.' He glanced at her. 'Do you think that's what's causing my illness—the fact that I had an insect bite? That's what my mates think.' His face contorted as another spasm of nausea washed over him and he struggled to overcome the urge to vomit. 'I didn't feel too bad until I arrived home in the U.K.,' he managed. 'I seem to have gone downhill ever since then. I've never felt as ill as this before.'

'It does seem quite likely that's what happened,' Amber told him. 'I'll do a biopsy, and take some blood for testing. Once we have a clear idea what we are dealing with, I'll be able to treat you more specifically.'

Jack looked worried. 'Some of my co-workers have been telling me that this sort of illness can be hard to treat. Some even said that people don't always recover. Is that true?'

'What kind of friends are these who say something like that?' Amber asked, raising a brow in astonishment. She gave him a reassuring smile. 'Let's wait until we have the results, shall we? What I will say is that I haven't lost a patient yet to an insect bite.'

Sarah mopped his brow with a cool flannel. 'She's right,' she said with a faint chuckle. 'We only bring in lay-consultants after we've been scratching our heads for a couple of weeks, because we reckon after that length of time anybody's guess is as good as ours.'

'You're making fun of me,' Jack said. He gave them a weak smile. 'You wouldn't be doing that if you felt the way I did.'

Sarah patted his hand. 'Only kidding,' she murmured. 'Dr Shaw knows what she's doing. She won't let you down.'

Amber made quick work of collecting the samples she needed. 'If it's true that you were bitten by a sandfly,' she said, 'especially a female sandfly, then it's quite possible that you have a parasitic infection. They can be really nasty and make you feel truly awful, because they attack your immune system and lower your resistance. If that's what has actually happened, we'll put a drip in your arm and treat you with a medication that will kill off the parasite. It won't happen overnight, though. Sometimes it can take several weeks for the treatment to take effect.'

Jack made a face. 'I'm not going anywhere in a hurry,' he said. 'I wouldn't have the energy.'

Amber left him with Sarah a few minutes later. She had been working for a good part of the day in A and E, but now it was time to go and check up on her patients on the surgical ward.

She called in on Martyn first of all. James was there, talking quietly to Caitlin, while Martyn was sitting in a chair at the side of his bed, balancing a laptop computer on his knees and frowning in concentration. He looked weary, a few lines of strain showing around his mouth and forehead, and Amber was immediately on the alert. James and Caitlin were oblivious to anything around them, smiling and sharing anecdotes with one another about life at university.

'I thought I'd drop by to see how you're getting

on,' Amber said, greeting Martyn and nodding towards James and Caitlin. 'I see you have company, though, so I'll make this a quick visit.'

James got to his feet. 'I've been looking for you all morning,' he murmured. He came over to her and gave her a hug. 'I heard about the job,' he said quietly. 'That was really bad news. I was so sure you would get it. The whole system is chaotic.'

'I suppose I can't complain,' she said. 'A lot of us are finding ourselves in the same boat, unfortunately.' It felt good to have his arms close gently around her. It was a light, comforting embrace that showed her he cared, but she couldn't help thinking it had come too late. A couple of days had passed since she had received the letter, and this was the first time he had mentioned the subject. She returned the embrace and then, much as she would have liked to prolong the contact, she gently broke away from him, turning her attention towards Martyn. It didn't seem right to be hugging, however brief and innocent the gesture, in front of a patient and his relative.

'I hear you've been trying to walk about a bit,'

she said, giving Martyn a brief look to try to assess how he was doing. 'That's good. Try to do things gradually, though. We don't want you to tax yourself too soon and end up having a relapse.' She frowned. 'Sarah tells me you've been making a lot of phone calls these last few days…and that's fine, if it's to keep you in touch with family and friends to generally cheer yourself up—only Sarah has the idea that you've been talking to people at the office and getting yourself into a state.'

He looked at her, very much like a little boy on the receiving end of a telling-off. 'It's just that I'm feeling so much better,' he said, using a placatory tone. 'And it's all down to your care and attention. You don't need to worry about me. I'm doing really well. You saved my life and I'm always going to be in your debt. I wouldn't dream of doing anything to undo all your good work.'

Amber sent him a knowing look. 'Don't even begin to think you can wind me around your little finger,' she admonished him. 'I'm onto your tricks. Your nephew warned me about you.'

'That was very well said.' Ethan's deep, male voice came from across the room, causing Amber to give a startled jump. She frowned at the screen that showed his image. Was that man forever going to be sneaking around and putting in an appearance when she least expected him?

She glanced at the watch on her wrist. 'Aren't you up and about again at an altogether unsociable hour?' she asked. Why couldn't he turn up when the night shift was on duty and she was safely out of the way? But perhaps he had always been an early riser…and that thought only added to her discomfort. What business did he have looking so fit and energetic when the sun was barely up in his part of the world?

'Do I detect sour grapes?' Ethan said, lifting a dark brow. 'I guess you've been hard at work for several hours by now. How is it that you're still looking after my uncle when your job is supposed to be in Accident and Emergency?'

'Professor Halloran asked me especially to look after Martyn,' she explained. 'But, in fact, my work is divided between A and E, the surgical ward and various other wards. I like it this way, because it gives me the chance to follow up on people who have been admitted to hospital from A and E. That doesn't usually happen with these senior house officer jobs, but I've found I really like being able to do that. It gives the training more depth, and that's why I applied for this particular rotation.'

'Didn't I hear you saying that you'd missed out on getting a job to go to after this one?' Martyn looked up from his laptop, a faint line indenting his brow. 'Most of the junior doctors' contracts come to an end soon, don't they?'

Amber sent him a fleeting glance. Although he had appeared to be engrossed in what he was doing, he had obviously been listening in to her earlier conversation with James.

'That's true,' she told him. 'Somebody mislaid my application and by the time it turned up, the job I applied for had been filled. Now it looks as though I'm going to be joining the ranks of the unemployed.'

Martyn shook his head. 'I don't know what

the world is coming to,' he said. 'Now, if I was in charge—'

'You'd be running us all around like a bee after honey,' Ethan interjected. He strode across the veranda of his property, his body long and lean, exuding health and vitality. 'You need to learn to take a back seat. Don't think I haven't heard about all the requests for changes at the plantation. You seem to forget that I'm in charge right now. I'll make the decisions so you don't need to worry about anything.'

'But you need me to guide you,' Martyn insisted. 'You haven't been involved with the day-to-day running of things up to now, and you have enough to do with the practice back home. You can't possibly do two full-time jobs, and if we don't get the new machinery up and running we'll be falling behind schedule.'

Practice? What practice would that be? Amber wondered, but Caitlin began to speak just then, diverting her thoughts. 'You know you shouldn't be getting involved with any of this,' Caitlin told him. 'Ethan is perfectly capable of dealing with everything. You just don't like to let go, do you?'

'It isn't that at all,' Martyn said, using an appeasing tone. 'It's just that I can see from all these work logs that the technicians haven't been on the site yet. We need them to service the equipment.' He nodded towards his laptop screen. 'Someone needs to gives them a nudge to get things moving.'

'So you've logged into the company's intranet, have you?' Ethan murmured. 'Is there no stopping you?' He was frowning, his blue eyes darkening like clouds rolling in off the sea. Behind him the sky was lit up with the glow of sunrise, colouring the landscape with a burst of flame-coloured light.

'I don't know what you mean,' Martyn said, assuming an innocent air. 'After all, I'm not back home at the plantation, or in the U.K. office, so I have to keep in touch with what's going on, one way or another.'

Amber walked over to him and peered down at the computer. 'This is a top-of–the-range laptop, isn't it?' she murmured, sounding impressed. 'A super-duper internet machine with all kinds of bells and whistles. May I take a closer look?' When he acknowledged her with a nod, she carefully placed her hands on the computer, turning it lightly so that she could see what was on the screen. 'Oh, so you're not using this for playing solitaire or amusing yourself with films...that's what you told Sarah you wanted the laptop for, wasn't it? But, then, you weren't exactly being upfront with her, were you?'

She looked sternly down at him and Martyn's face took on a faintly sheepish look. 'I do want to do those things. It's just that I haven't quite found the time just yet.'

'Well, I'm afraid it's too late now, because your office is closing, as of this minute,' she informed him. With one swift movement Amber lifted the computer from him and closed the lid. 'I'm confiscating this,' she said, moving away from him. 'You'll get it back when I've decided you've had sufficient rest.'

'You can't do that,' Martyn protested, his jaw

dropping open. Clearly, no one had ever thwarted him in such a way before.

'Can't I?' She studied him thoughtfully. 'I believe I just did.'

She heard a stifled chuckle and glanced in the direction of the video link. 'I do believe he's finally met his match,' Ethan said, giving her an appreciative look. He made a thumbs-up sign. 'Perhaps Professor Halloran wasn't so far off beam in keeping you in charge here after all,' he added in a musing tone. 'I had wanted to bring in our own consultant, and I'd have gone ahead and done it if Martyn hadn't vetoed me.'

Martyn glowered at both of them. 'I may yet change my mind,' he threatened. 'I'm sure I have the number of one or two specialists who can be relied on to do things my way.'

Amber wasn't fazed by his reaction. 'By all means go ahead,' she said. 'You still won't get your computer back until you've had a good, long rest.'

Caitlin put a hand to her mouth, but whether that was to cover her amusement, or to hide the extent of her shock, Amber wasn't sure. Either way, James lightly touched the girl's arm and murmured, 'I have to go back to work now. It's good to see that you're bearing up well.' He nodded towards Ethan. 'You can rely on Amber to take care of things. She's always been a force to be reckoned with.'

He smiled at Amber, and went with her to the door as she sought to find a safe place for the laptop. 'Are we on for lunch later today?' he asked.

She nodded. 'That would be good.' She looked at him closely, but she couldn't read his expression and she wasn't at all sure what was going on with him lately. Perhaps he wasn't able to decide what he really wanted. He seemed to be blowing hot and cold, but then again who was she to judge? These days her emotions were a mishmash of confusion and disappointment, only enlivened every now and again by one of his smiles.

Once she had disposed safely of the laptop into a secure locker, she went back to Martyn's private room. Caitlin had gone to get herself a cup of coffee, and Martyn was alone, still sitting in the chair by the bed.

'I need to check your blood pressure,' Amber said, and Martyn obligingly held out his arm, though he still had a disgruntled look on his face. Amber stared about her to see if Ethan was still online, but the screen was blank, and she wasn't sure whether she felt relief or disappointment about that.

'He's gone to work,' Martyn said, following her gaze. 'Like you, he's a doctor, only he has a private practice within the main hospital back home. He trained in emergency medicine. It's all he ever really wanted to do, but he has other interests besides that, including half-ownership of the plantation. Until now he's been a silent partner.' He gave a faint scowl. 'Only, just lately, he's starting to have a lot more to say for himself on that score.'

A doctor… That probably explained a lot, Amber mused. Ethan would understand only too well what was happening with his uncle. It was no wonder that he wanted the very best care for him, knowing how very ill he was.

'That's because he cares about you, and doesn't want you to over-extend yourself,' she told him as she wrapped the blood-pressure cuff around his arm. 'He said he'll sort things out, and perhaps you should let him get on with it without trying to interfere.'

'And what would you know about running a pineapple plantation?' Martyn said grumpily. 'My grandfather started the project, and I have to keep up the family tradition. There's more to it than simply planting seeds and harvesting the crop. If we don't keep up to date with our research projects, we won't be able to develop new varieties of fruit, and our produce will become vulnerable to the ravages of pests and diseases.' He gave her a mournful look. 'That's why I need my computer back, or, at the very least, my mobile phone.'

'All in good time,' Amber said in a peaceful tone. 'Nothing major is going to happen in the next few hours, except that you're going to lie back and relax. I'll switch the TV on for you, if you like, and you can amuse yourself with the afternoon film or a house make-over programme. It's what you need, something pleasant and un-challenging to send you to sleep.'

'I don't want to watch a film,' he said in a terse voice.

'You can't go on the way you did before.' She indicated the blood-pressure monitor. 'Look at that,' she commanded him. 'The reading is way too high. You've just miraculously come through a very difficult and worrying time, and you're not doing anything to help yourself.'

'Is everyone in your family the same as you?' he asked, narrowing his eyes. 'Is there a stroppy gene mixed in somewhere with all the usual ones?'

'I'm not altogether sure about that,' Amber murmured, releasing the cuff. 'My father is ef-ficient, hard-working, always striving to do better, but he's generally easy to get along with. My mother is usually very calm and sensible, though she does have her moments when she decides enough is enough and makes her feelings clear to everyone around her.'

She frowned at him. 'I know exactly what she

would say to you right now… "Nature, time and patience…three great physicians. Let them do their work.'"

'Hmm.' Martyn studied her curiously as she put away the monitor. 'That's quite an unusual saying, isn't it?'

'Is it?' Amber raised a brow. 'My mother says it all the time.' Perhaps they didn't use that phrase where he came from.

His gaze trailed over her features. 'Does she look at all like you? Your hair colour and all those natural curls are something quite out of the ordinary, aren't they? Perhaps you've inherited them from her?'

'Well, from the pictures I've seen of her as a young woman, we're very much alike. Some people have commented that we could have been mistaken for twins if all you had to go on were the photographs.' She frowned as she reached for his chart. 'I'm going to add another lot of tablets to your regimen,' she said. 'We need to get that blood pressure down.'

'Is your mother a medical professional, the same

as you?' He was looking at her thoughtfully, and she guessed his interest was caught because he liked to know about people in general. Perhaps that was what gave him an edge in the business world—that, and a tendency to overwork.

'No. My father is a GP, as it happens, and I suppose it was being around him and seeing how much he helped people that made me want to go into medicine. My mother is a graphic artist. She's very talented—she studied in London initially, and then she found work with an advertising company. They used to have their premises quite close to where your offices are situated now, come to think of it…only, that was years ago, before I was born. Your place wasn't built back then, was it?'

He shook his head. 'We moved into the Docklands building a few years ago. We were always based locally, though.'

'Well, I don't think my mother really liked working in the city, and eventually she decided to move to Henley-on-Thames. In fact, it was when she moved there that she met my father.

They had a whirlwind courtship by all accounts, and were married within a very short time, a matter of a few weeks, I heard.'

'Do you have any brothers or sisters?'

'No.' She was pensive for a moment or two. 'I've always thought it would be nice to be part of a big family, but it didn't happen. I think my mother had problems when she gave birth to me, and perhaps that's why she didn't have any more children. I was born prematurely, and I think both my parents were a little shocked that they had a child within that first year of marriage. My father said it seemed like no sooner were they married than they had to set about preparing a nursery. At least they don't seem to hold it against me.' She gave him a quick grin, and in return his features relaxed and his eyes took on a glimmer of amusement.

'And look at you now...totally in command and still ruling the roost. You're not going to give in and let me have my technology back any time soon, are you? I could really do with having my mobile phone.'

She shook her head. 'Definitely not for a while. I want you to get well again, and there's no point in you blustering,' she said. 'Ethan and Caitlin warned me that you'd be too much to handle, but I don't believe it for a minute. You might growl and snarl a little, but you're a pussycat really, aren't you?'

He smiled. 'You've seen through me,' he said. Then he reached out and grasped her hand when she would have moved away from the chair. 'Sit down on the bed near to me and talk to me for a while, will you, if you have time? It's very boring in here, you know, and you're such a sweet girl, an angel to look at, and you brighten my day like nothing else. Tell me about your family life…where you lived, where you grew up.'

She smiled back at him and obligingly sat down. Sarah would page her if any problems cropped up and nothing urgent was happening right this minute, as far as she could tell. 'I grew up in Henley-on-Thames,' she said. 'It was all very peaceful, and my mother managed to do some of her work from home, which was great.

Then my father started his own medical practice and we lived on the premises. Over the years the practice grew and he took on partners.'

'It sounds idyllic. Your father must be very proud of you, having achieved so much. I know you're a very good doctor. I've seen it for myself, and everyone says so.' He didn't let go of her hand, but stroked it gently as though reassuring himself that she was real, flesh and blood.

'Am I interrupting something?' Ethan's voice cracked like a pistol shot across the room.

Amber gave a faint gasp and swivelled around to glower at the screen. 'So you're back again,' she murmured. 'I thought you had gone off to work. How is your uncle supposed to get any rest when you keep popping up every few minutes?'

Ethan's eyes narrowed on her. 'So I *am* interrupting.' He nodded, as though confirming an inner thought. 'That's interesting. You seem inordinately put out by me being around, in virtual form if not in the flesh.'

'Perhaps I am,' she answered tautly. 'It's very offputting to have you appear out of nowhere like that every so often and, besides, all that, as I've explained to you in detail, Martyn needs to rest.'

Okay, so Ethan *was* a relative, and visiting hours in the hospital were fairly lax, but there had to be a limit as to how much her nerves were to be put through their paces, surely? Who else would stand for it? Not Professor Halloran, that was for sure, though he would never be around long enough to put it to the test.

'He isn't likely to get much rest with you holding his hand that way, is he?' Ethan's gaze was full of censure, and Amber felt a surge of guilt sweep over her. What was he implying? She wasn't doing anything wrong and in, fact, it was Martyn who was holding her hand, but perhaps from where Ethan was standing it looked suspicious. 'His blood pressure's already high, according to the nurse,' Ethan added, 'and any time now it's likely to be off the charts.'

Amber glanced at Martyn, expecting him to rush to her defence, but he was chuckling softly. 'Children,' he said in a droll tone, looking from one to the other, 'let's not have any bickering, please. It isn't good for the patient to be caught in the middle, now, is it?'

'Oh, you're impossible. You're both as bad as one another.' Amber withdrew her hand from Martyn's grasp and got to her feet. 'He'd probably recover much faster if he was left in peace for a while,' she informed Ethan curtly, 'without you coming on line to constantly remind him of all the work issues that are floating around. I suggest you limit your video meetings to prearranged times.'

'And if I don't?' Ethan's brows rose.

'Then I might just arrange for the video link to be cut from this end,' she said. 'I doubt either of you would want that.'

Martyn glanced at Ethan, a glimmer lighting his eyes. 'Feisty, isn't she? Beware the woman who doesn't embrace technology,' he warned.

Ethan gave a short laugh. 'I've battled with worse opponents,' he countered. 'Besides, I'm the one who has Professor Halloran's loyalty and support, so I'm not likely to worry about empty threats, am I?' He placed his hands palms flat against the back of his hips and proceeded to lightly stretch his spine, looking every inch the cock of the walk, much to Amber's annoyance.

'Anyway,' he added, 'I just came back to say I've spoken with the manager at the plantation, and he says they're on the ball with the seed development programme, so you needn't have any worries on that score. And the technicians will be along to service the new equipment this morning.'

'So now—' he broke off to direct his remarks towards Amber '—I shall go off and begin my stint at the hospital. I shall come back on line first thing in the morning…your morning, my evening. I doubt I'll be in any mood to do battle by then, but don't count on it.'

Amber's green eyes flashed, shooting sparks at the screen, but Ethan cut the link, leaving her to vent her frustration inwardly. She turned back to Martyn. 'Obviously the "I'm in charge" gene is fully functional in your family, or is it just the males that possess it?' Caitlin obviously didn't, from what Amber could glean, because she was soft and vulnerable, the kind of woman who wanted to know that there was a man around to take care of her.

Martyn laughed softly. 'Ethan's all right, once you get to know him. He tends to be a bit guarded about women having designs on the family fortune, but that's only because both he and I have experienced the unfortunate side of opposite-sex relationships. For my part, women seemed to want to comfort me after my wife died, but I could see perfectly well through those that had an ulterior motive, and to be honest, no one could ever replace my beloved Grace.'

He was thoughtful for a moment. 'As to Ethan, women tend to be a little more subtle in their approach. If his mother was alive, I dare say she would set him straight on their various whiles, but unfortunately both his parents were killed in a boating accident when he was in his teens. I think it's made him tougher, in a way. He's found his own path in life, and he hasn't done too badly for it.'

'Caitlin said that you took care of him. I expect that means he's more like a brother to her than a cousin.'

'Yes, that's true. That's why he looks out for her all the time. Of course, it wasn't just me who took care of him. Grace was like a second mother to him. Unfortunately, we lost her a few years back, when she had a bad asthma attack. I'm pretty sure that's why Ethan took up medicine…he watched Grace battle with asthma and he wanted to learn how to make a difference in people's lives.'

'I'm sorry. You must miss her dearly.' Amber's words were heartfelt. He looked and spoke like a man who had cared deeply for his wife.

'Yes, I do.'

The nurse came to bring him his medication just then, and Amber decided it was time to take her leave. 'I need to go and look in on my other patients,' she said. 'Behave yourself, and don't think you can wheedle the nurses into giving you your computer back. It isn't going to happen.' She gave the nurse a meaningful look, and the girl nodded.

'You can rely on me,' she said. 'Sarah's been telling me all about his workaholic ways. She said we should put a note in his file to warn everyone.'

'What a great idea,' Amber agreed. 'I'll go and do it right now.' She grinned in Martyn's direction, and as she left the room she heard him complaining to the nurse about people who took it on themselves to dictate his life.

Martyn was a good man, but he needed someone to be firm with him and ensure that he lived to fight another day. Ethan was doing his best for him, trying to put his mind at ease, but there was only so much he could do from a distance. She had been wrong to condemn him for coming back and forth on line, but the man made her jumpy, putting her on edge every time he came into view, and she had no idea why she should feel that way.

CHAPTER FOUR

OVER the next few days, Martyn's condition improved steadily. He would never be the active man he once was, but there was more colour in his cheeks now, and his breathing was much easier as the medication helped ease the congestion in his lungs.

'When is he going to be able to leave hospital?' Ethan asked one day, when Martyn had been taken to the X-ray unit for follow-up checks, and Amber was sitting by his bed, writing up his medical notes.

'I would say that he should stay here for at least another week,' Amber told him, 'and then he would be better off having a couple of weeks in rehab. He's quite shaky on his feet and he needs physiotherapy to help him regain his strength.'

'But you won't have anything to do with what goes on in the rehabilitation unit, will you?' Ethan said, giving her a quick look.

It seemed an odd question for him to ask. 'I'll be able to check up on his progress from time to time,' Amber replied, 'but you're right, there will be other doctors in charge over there.' She studied him. 'Why do you ask? Are you still concerned about my involvement in his care?' She had thought he had grown used to her being around, and that he had finally accepted that she was the one making the day-to-day decisions in consultation with Professor Halloran.

'You've looked after him very well. I've no complaints on that score. What concerns me is that you and he seem to be growing closer by the day,' Ethan murmured. 'I'm not sure what to make of that. Video links have their limitations after all, but I do know that my uncle is taking a very special interest in you.'

'I don't know why you should think that way, and I'm sorry you feel it's a problem,' she said. 'I like your uncle. He's a thoughtful and considerate man, and he always thinks of others, even when he's struggling to manage things for himself.'

'He certainly thinks about you a lot.' He studied her fleetingly, as though trying to work something out in his head. 'He seems concerned that you have no job to go to when you finish your contract here. I don't see why that should be his problem, do you?' His gaze seemed to home in on her very much as though he had a target in his sights.

Amber was taken aback by his comments. 'It isn't anything that he should be worried about, obviously,' she answered on a cautious note. 'Anyway, I don't believe he thinks about me all the time, any more than he does about other people.'

'He's very curious about you. In between bombarding me with questions about the business, and making suggestions for ways we can advertise our products, all he wants is to sing your praises to me. I've not seen him this animated in quite a while.'

Amber gave that some thought. 'He's certainly been using his phone a good deal lately, so much so that I've had to threaten to confiscate it again. He may have been trying to contact advertising agencies, now I come to think of it, but I don't believe his fever of activity is all to do with business. I know he's been talking to friends.'

In fact, she thought he had on occasion been talking to an investigative agency of some sort… She had overheard the odd snatch of conversation from time to time when she had walked into his room, though he usually finished the call when she approached. Perhaps he was checking into the background of a prospective employee. 'I just have the feeling that he is a very compassionate man who cares about everyone and everything.'

'That's true.' Ethan nodded. 'He's always been that way. Grace used to say he had a heart big enough to embrace the world, and sometimes she worried that people would take advantage of him.'

Amber could see how that might happen. 'Perhaps he can't help himself,' she murmured. 'He asks me about my other patients, and he's even been wandering down the corridor to visit one of them whenever he feels up to it—a man who went down with a parasitic infection. I've been able to follow up on the man more closely because I was the one who initially liaised with the tropical diseases unit.'

She frowned. 'Martyn seemed quite worried about how Jack was doing, and I wondered if it was something that he had ever suffered from, though I can't find anything in his notes to that effect.'

'I have the feeling it was more that he was impressed by your ability to diagnose the condition in the first place, given that you're a fairly junior doctor. He told me all about it. He seems to think that other people might have missed the diagnosis, but, then again, he isn't a medical man. I guess he's interested in Jack because he's done lots of interesting things on his travels. Oh, and he said he was curious to know if you had studied tropical medicine.'

'He has been asking a lot of questions, hasn't he?' Amber smiled up at the screen. 'I did think about it at one time, as another string to my bow, you might say. I thought it might come in useful if I ever travelled the world, but other things got in the way. I decided that I was really interested in accident and emergency work, and I pinned my hopes on specialising in that. Then the job fell through, as you know.'

'So you still don't know what you'll be doing when you finish there?'

She shook her head, causing a ripple of curls to quiver and dance in chaotic disorder. 'I don't have a clue. I asked my father if he had any vacancies at the surgery, but things seem to be running very smoothly there and they can't afford to take on anyone else.'

Sarah came into the room just then, and Amber finished making the notes in the file before standing up.

'Is there a problem, Sarah?'

'Not really. It's just that Jack's ultrasound results have come back and I think you need to take a look at them. His liver and spleen are enlarged, so it looks as though the treatment's not working as effectively as you hoped.'

'All right. I'll come and see what's to be done. There is another treatment, but I would have preferred not to use it unless it was really necessary. There are some toxic side-effects that can affect the kidneys, so I need to be very careful how I administer the drug, and he'll need to be monitored very closely.'

She glanced towards the computer screen, taking in Ethan's brooding stare. 'I expect I'll talk to you again later,' she said. She was getting a little more used to him constantly being around, and there were even times she found herself looking forward to seeing him. It was only when he questioned her motives, albeit in a roundabout way, that she began to feel aggrieved.

He nodded. 'Later.'

Jack was still very unwell, and it was a worry knowing that his liver and spleen were affected. Amber explained to him about the new medication, and with his permission she began to set it up. It would take time before it worked its magic, and Amber waited anxiously for results.

Another week passed by, and very gradually she began to see a change in the young man. 'It looks as though we've cracked it at last,' she told him as she checked through the latest batch of blood test results.

Jack smiled. He looked much better than he had previously, and Amber was pleased to see a sparkle back in his eyes.

'Your girlfriend is going to be so thrilled when she comes to see you at visiting time,' she said. 'It'll take a few more weeks of treatment until you're properly clear, but you're definitely on the way.'

'It's brilliant news. My parents are going to be over the moon, as well.' He was still smiling. 'They've been worried sick about me.'

Amber left him to absorb his good fortune and went off in search of James. She just had to share this with him. Every day they came together to talk about the highs and lows of their work, and this was definitely a high.

'I saw him go into the patients' day room a few minutes ago,' Sarah said. 'He told me he was looking for one of his asthma patients but, to be honest, I think the room has been empty for the last hour. Martyn sometimes ambles down there in the late afternoon, but he was waiting for Ethan to get in touch last I heard.'

'Thanks, Sarah,' Amber murmured. 'I'll go and check in there first of all.'

There was a spring in her step as she walked down the corridor and hurried towards the room. Martyn would be glad to hear the news, too, because he had kept up his interest in Jack's case, wanting to know if the side effects had caused any problems. Luckily, they hadn't.

She pushed open the door to the day room. James was in there, though his back was towards her, and as soon as she saw his lean, familiar figure, she brightened. But then he half turned and with a shock she realised that he was not alone.

Caitlin was there with him, and they had their arms around one another, locked in an intimate embrace. He was kissing her, but as they heard the sound of the door opening, they broke apart.

Amber stared from one to the other, her heart taking a downward leap in her chest, her throat closing in a surge of emotion. Then she swivelled around and hurried out of the room.

Her worst fears had come crashing down on her, and she had no idea what to do or how to cope.

'Is something wrong?' Martyn asked. He was walking slowly along the corridor towards her and now there was a look of concern on his face. 'What is it? Has something happened to a patient? Is it Jack? Has he taken a turn for the worse?'

She looked up at him, unable to speak for a moment or two. Then, 'Jack's fine,' she told him briefly. 'He's absolutely fine. His treatment's working.'

Martyn turned to follow the direction she was taking. 'Will you slow down?' he asked. 'Where are you going?'

She didn't answer him, but at that moment Caitlin and James came out of the day room, and on hearing their voices Martyn half turned with her to look towards them.

James looked pale, his features sombre, but Caitlin's face still wore the bemused look of a girl who didn't know what was happening in the world around her.

'Will you walk me back to my room?' Martyn

said, looking at Amber. 'I'm feeling a bit shaky. I was going to watch TV in the day room, but I think I've changed my mind. I've just remembered that there's racing on the radio, and I'd rather listen to that in my room.'

'Yes, of course,' Amber said. The last thing she wanted right now was to have company of any kind, but Martyn was a patient, and his needs had to come first. They started to walk along the corridor, leaving James and Caitlin behind. Perhaps James thought better of following her, seeing that she wasn't alone. The relief Amber felt was small consolation.

'Are you still worrying about finding a job?' Martyn asked once they were back in his room. 'You haven't seemed to be your usual self these last few days. I know you've been concerned about Jack not improving as fast as you would have liked, but you're doing all you can for him, aren't you?'

Amber helped him into his chair. He sounded as though he was having difficulty breathing, and she guessed that the effort of walking to the day room had placed a strain on his heart. 'Just you try to relax for a while, and get your breath back,' she said. She poured him a drink of juice from the jug on his bedside table, and offered him a tablet to dissolve on his tongue and ease the spasm of pain in his chest.

He accepted both, and then leaned back in his chair, gathering his strength.

'Jack is feeling much better,' she told him. 'The treatment seems to be working at last, and we've managed to keep the side effects down to a minimum. With any luck, he'll be going home at the end of the month.'

'That's brilliant news.' Colour was gradually coming back into Martyn's cheeks, and Amber watched him, concerned for his well-being and trying to push the image of James and Caitlin out of her mind.

Seeing them together that way had come as a tremendous shock, but now, as she slowly absorbed the reality of the situation, she was trying to analyse how she truly felt.

Was it something she had known all along—

that she and James had drifted apart? Would it have happened even if Caitlin had not come along? What was it that James had said? '*You can rely on Amber to take care of things. She's always been a force to be reckoned with.*'

Perhaps that's where the trouble lay. She was self reliant up to a point, whereas Caitlin was young and vulnerable, and she brought out the protective instinct in James. It didn't matter that Amber might be filled with self-doubt from time to time. She tried her best to deal with each problem as it came along, and it was a matter of pride to her that she should try sort things out for herself instead of wearing her heart on her sleeve. But maybe James didn't want a woman who was on equal terms with him, and that was a sad truth that Amber was trying to take on board.

Her shoulders slumped. She was empty inside. There was nothing left. No dreams to cherish, no soul mate to walk hand in hand with her through life, no job to help her seek solace in helping others…no future. All that lay before her was an endless, bleak desert.

Martyn stirred, and she realised that he was studying her thoughtfully as he shifted in his chair. His condition was beginning to improve, and she could see that he was frowning, preoccupied now that he was feeling a little more rested.

'Would you like me to switch the radio on for you?' she asked. The headphones were on a hook on the wall behind him and she made to reach for them, but he shook his head.

'I've changed my mind,' he said. 'I don't feel like listening to the radio after all.' He pulled in a deep, steadying breath. 'I'm glad Jack is feeling better. It will be good for him to go home.' He hesitated. 'I keep wondering what's going to happen when I go back home—back to Hawaii, I mean. Life is never going to be the same for me again, is it? I'm beginning to realise that I might struggle in some ways without help. Here in hospital it's reassuring to know that someone is always on hand to help out, but I won't be able to rely on that back home, will I?'

'You'll have Ethan, won't you?' Amber frowned. 'He's a doctor, and he's your nephew…

he isn't going to leave you to cope on your own, is he?'

'He has enough to do, with the plantation and his work at the hospital. I can't ask him to do any more.'

'What about Caitlin? Her university course finishes soon, doesn't it? Won't she be on hand to take care of you?'

Martyn pulled a face. 'She's very young, and she has her life ahead of her. I can't ask her to stay home and look after me. Besides, she plans to take up a post in pharmaceutical sciences at the university hospital in Oahu. Her exam results here in London have been excellent, and she's assured of a place there.'

Amber shook her head. 'I don't understand how you can be feeling concerned about what will happen back home. In your circumstances, you could have someone take care of you twenty-four hours a day…though I can't see you putting up with that state of affairs for very long. I don't think you're temperamentally suited to have someone by your side for that length of time.'

Martyn began to smile. 'You understand me so well, don't you? And how long have we known each other? A very short time.' He was thoughtful for a while, and then said, 'Of course, there is a solution to my problem. You would be my perfect choice…who could be better to look out for me?'

Amber stared at him. 'I'm not sure that I follow your drift,' she said.

Martyn leaned forward in his chair, his face brightening as though everything was becoming clear to him. 'It's like this… It occurs to me that with you being out of work, you might just want to think about coming over to Hawaii to take care of me—on a part-time basis,' he hurried to add. 'I wouldn't want you to feel that you needed to be there all the time. You could always take up a part-time post at the hospital. I have contacts that could fix you up with work. I know they're short of people in the emergency unit.'

Amber was stunned by his proposition. 'But there must be all sorts of people you could ask to do that,' she said, 'people who live near to you back home.'

'Possibly,' he agreed. 'But I know you, and I like you. I've become very fond of you over these last few weeks. More to the point, I trust you, Amber. Think of it as a great opportunity. Not only could you work in Emergency, you could learn more about medicine in a different country, a different climate.' He watched her as though he was trying to gauge her reaction. Then he leaned forward and reached for her hand, clasping it between his palms. 'Couldn't you do with a break right now...sun...sand...sea...? What could be better?'

'I... You've taken me completely by surprise,' Amber managed. 'I don't know what to say.'

'Say yes,' Martyn urged her. 'You don't have any reason to stay here, do you? Except your family, of course. But we could arrange for you to link up online, or even for them to come out to see you.'

'I don't know.' Amber was frowning, trying to take it all in. What was there for her here, except heartbreak and unemployment? Her whole life had changed over these last few weeks. Her career would soon be on hold, and this very afternoon her love life had come crashing down around her. Why shouldn't she take the easy way out and try to escape the tragedy? Wouldn't it be the chance of a lifetime to go and work on a tropical island in the Pacific Ocean?

'Well then, let's say that you come out for six months, to give it a try? That way you wouldn't be committing yourself for ever. What do you think?'

'What does she think about what?' Ethan's voice broke the silence, crackling through the air and slicing through Amber's reverie like a knife. 'Am I missing something? Why are you two holding hands again?' His voice was etched with suspicion and his blue eyes raked over her, so that Amber felt her defences spring up in an act of self-preservation.

Why was he so concerned about her relationship with his uncle? Did he really think she was trying to inveigle her way into his uncle's heart? It hurt that he should think so little of her.

'Your uncle has just offered me a job in Hawaii,' she said. Her jaw lifted. 'And I'm thinking of accepting it.'

Ethan gasped, but Martyn's hands tightened on hers, and a smile lit up his face. 'You won't regret it if you do, I promise you.'

She smiled at him. 'We'll see. Just give me a little while to think things through,' she said. 'I'm not sure that making snap decisions is a good idea.'

'I know you'll make the right choice.' Martyn was irrepressible now, and she could see he believed it was a done deal. That gave her pause for thought. It was one thing to rile Ethan by making rash statements on the spur of the moment, but Martyn deserved better. His offer was genuine, she was sure of that, because he wanted the best for both of them, and it would only be fair to give the idea due consideration.

Ethan, on the other hand, was ready to take issue with her on the mere suggestion that she and Martyn were cooking up plans between them.

She gazed across the room at the screen. Ethan's gaze drilled into her, and she could feel the frustration that fed the flame that burned in his eyes. Did he think she had manoeuvred Martyn into offering her this opportunity?

That was his problem, she decided. She'd had enough of being let down by men and the system in general. It was time to take charge of her life, instead of allowing events to buffet her here and there in whimsical fashion. If Ethan didn't like the option she chose, that was unfortunate. Martyn was offering her a way out, and she would give his suggestion some serious, deep thought.

CHAPTER FIVE

'I CAN'T wait to be back on the island,' Martyn said, 'but it shouldn't be much longer now, all being well.' In the background, the quiet drone of the plane's engines seemed to confirm what he was saying. 'Of course, the delay at the start of the flight didn't help, did it? Though I expect we'd have had to wait much longer if you hadn't stepped in and helped the flight attendant.'

'I felt sorry for her,' Amber murmured. 'There isn't really any treatment for a perforated eardrum, except for painkillers and maybe antibiotics. But she certainly wasn't able to come with us on the flight in that condition, so it left the airport authorities with a problem to solve, didn't it? They had to quickly find someone to replace her.'

Martyn pulled in a long, deep breath. 'It all turned out fine in the end, though, thank goodness. And now we're on the last leg of the journey.' He smiled softly. 'It seems such an age since I last set foot on Hawaiian soil, and yet really it's only been a few months.'

'Perhaps it feels that way because so much has happened to you in that time,' Amber suggested. 'You've been very ill.' She frowned. 'In fact, I was worried in case you wouldn't be well enough to fly, but you seem to have surprised us all.'

'I was determined to make it,' he said with quiet satisfaction. 'I have to go home. I don't know how much longer I have on this earth, but I want to die on Hawaiian soil.'

Amber reached for his hand and gave it a gentle squeeze. 'Please don't say that. You've been doing so well.'

'Only with your help,' he said. 'You mustn't worry about me. I'm content. I'm glad that I've been given a little more time.' He gave her an appreciative, gentle smile, before leaning back in his seat and slowly closing his eyes. Within minutes, he appeared to have drifted into a light doze.

Amber gazed out of the window of the plane. She still found it hard to believe that she was actually sitting here by his side, getting ready for the approach to the island. Her mother's warnings and the echo of her parental anxiety were still ringing loud and clear in her head.

'But it's so far away, and you don't know this man or these people,' her mother had said.

'Why don't you speak to Martyn yourself?' Amber had suggested. 'I'm sure he'll be able to put your mind at ease.' Her mother had agreed to do that, but in fact her father had made his own checks to see that all was well. He had spoken to the hospital authorities on the island and verified that the job she was going to did indeed exist, and though Amber protested that she was perfectly able to take care of herself, she was pleased that they cared enough to make sure that she would be safe.

Her mother was still agitated, even after she had spoken to Martyn. 'This is all so sudden,' she said, 'and I can't think why he wants to take you halfway across the world.' For a moment Amber thought she sounded very much like Ethan. Ethan was definitely guarded about Martyn's sudden decision to ask her to come to Hawaii with him, and she still had the feeling he thought she might somehow have manipulated his uncle into taking this action.

'Are you sure you know what you're doing?' he quizzed her, his blue eyes narrowing on her. 'My uncle might be physically frail, but he won't be alone out here. Hawaii is my land, my territory, and my family is everything to me. I won't stand by and see any of them hurt.' It was a warning she took to heart. She didn't blame Ethan for his attitude... it was good that he cared so much for his uncle, but it was unnerving to know that he was suspicious of her motives. Clearly she couldn't look forward to everything being plain sailing when she arrived in Hawaii.

As to her mother, Amber couldn't quite see what she was worried about. 'Everything's been properly sorted out,' she told her. 'The arrangement is that I'll have my own house—well, it's a bungalow, really—but it will be fairly close to the big house where Martyn lives. I'm not sure whether his nephew lives with him, but I think it was Ethan's idea that I have my own place.' He didn't want her getting too close to Martyn, that was for sure, but she wasn't about to say that to her mother and cause her to worry even more.

'Aren't you surprised that Martyn has taken to you this way?' her mother asked. 'He's given you no real reason for wanting you to go out there, has he?'

'He's set up a job for me,' Amber said. 'Perhaps he was concerned that I was going to be unemployed. Anyway, I start work at the hospital two weeks after I arrive in Oahu.'

At least, after talking to Martyn, her mother was no longer putting obstacles in her way. She seemed reconciled to the fact that Amber had made up her mind, and she seemed slightly appeased when Amber promised to stay in touch.

'I want you to talk to me every week, and tell me what's going on,' her mother said. 'We'll set up one of those video cam links that you told me about.'

'I'll do it as soon as I get there,' Amber said. 'Honestly, you're worrying over nothing. Didn't you feel reassured after you spoke to Martyn? He's really a very good man, you know. Dad spoke to him on the phone, didn't he? And he didn't have any problem with him.'

Her mother was still fretting. 'He spoke to his nephew, too, but he didn't seem too keen on the idea. I'm just taken aback by the whole thing. This has all happened so quickly,' she said. 'I can't get used to the idea.'

That was the only explanation her mother gave for her anxiety, and Amber did her best to set her mind at rest. Her mother didn't usually react this way to new situations and Amber thought it a little odd that she should be so unsettled about it even now.

'You'll be able to come and visit me, won't you?' Amber murmured. 'You and Dad are due a holiday, and I'll be back after six months anyway.'

'So you say. He said you could stay on, didn't he?'

'Either way,' Amber said softly, 'we'll find a

way to keep in touch on a regular basis and we'll meet up after a few months.'

Ethan's attitude didn't surprise her. He was the one person who was still not reconciled to the situation in any way, and Amber was uncertain how she was going to deal with him. He had said he would meet them at the airport, and already she was bracing herself to cope with that.

Martyn stirred in the seat beside her. 'Caitlin asked me to ring her as soon as we arrived. We're running late, though, aren't we, with the delay at the airport? I expect she'll be working herself up into a state, wondering what's happened.'

'I'm sure she'll be fine. She strikes me as a fairly level-headed young woman.' She glanced at him. 'Are you all right? You look a little pale. Are you worried because you've left Caitlin behind?'

'Not really,' Martyn said. 'I just don't want her to be anxious, that's all. She was apprehensive about my leaving, and a little concerned about not coming with me, but I knew she wanted to stay on in the U.K. for a few weeks more, and I gave her my blessing.' He smiled and patted her hand. 'I'm just a little tired, that's all…nothing to worry about. I shall be fine once I'm home. I'm really looking forward to it.'

Amber sat back in her seat and tried to relax. Caitlin had stayed behind to finish off her last few weeks at university, although in truth her exams were behind her, and there was no real need for her to remain. James was the reason she had decided not to come home. She didn't want to tear herself away from him, and he was only too happy to have her around for as long as possible.

'I'm so sorry, Amber,' he had said. 'I don't know how it happened. I think the world of you, you know I do. I was in love with you, and then Caitlin came into my life and all at once everything was topsy-turvy.'

Amber wasn't sure any longer how she felt about the situation. She had thought she loved him, but now that it was over, her heart was still in one piece and there was just a numb feeling where once she used to care.

She looked out of the window at the landscape below. Right now, they were flying over beautiful coral reefs on the approach to the island of Oahu. The sea was a startling, vivid blue, the surf lapped at the edges of Oahu's golden Waikiki beach, and looming up ahead of them was Diamond Head, the crater of an extinct volcano, magnificent with its ridges and steep rock faces. Calcite crystals glimmered in the sunshine, sparkling like the jewels that gave the crater its name, and the sun overhead gave the rim of the crater a golden glow.

'That mountain range is the Koolau Range,' Martyn said, pointing out the peaks in the far distance. 'Soon we'll be coming into Honolulu airport.'

Amber felt her heartbeat quicken. Would Ethan be there to meet them, as he had promised?

Martyn was using a wheelchair, so they were last to get off the plane, but everything about the disembarkation procedure was made smooth for them, and it was only a short time later that they found themselves in the passenger greeting area.

Amber thought she might have trouble picking out Ethan among the crowd, but he was the one who found them, and he came towards them, his stride long and brisk. He was much taller than she had expected, and altogether he made an impressive figure. His skin was lightly bronzed, his hair midnight black, and he was wearing cool, casual clothes, light-coloured trousers and a blue shirt, worn loosely so that it skimmed his hips. He had with him a straw-coloured canvas holdall.

'It's good to see you again, Martyn,' he said, placing the bag over the backrest of the wheelchair and reaching out to clasp his uncle's arms in greeting. 'You look much better than I had expected. Did you manage to get plenty of rest on the journey?'

'I did.' Martyn smiled. 'It all went very well…but, then, I had Amber to look after me.' He glanced in Amber's direction, and Ethan turned and took a step towards her.

'Amber… *Aloha*,' he said. He reached for her, his large hands closing around her arms in a firm but gentle grip. 'Welcome to my homeland. I must thank you for taking such good care of my uncle.' He released her, adding, 'I have something for you.' Then he turned for a moment and took a small package from the canvas bag. Opening it, he drew out a perfect white orchid, before dropping the packaging back into the bag. 'A beautiful flower for a lovely young woman,' he said, slipping it into her hair just behind her right ear.

His gaze travelled over her, taking in the soft lines of the dress she was wearing, a sleeveless, gently flowing affair that was designed to keep her cool. 'You're even more exotic than I could ever have imagined. It was one thing seeing you on a computer screen, day by day, but here, in the flesh, is something else entirely. You're a knockout, an astonishingly beautiful young woman.'

Then, before she could even draw breath, he reached for her once more, tugging her towards him, his arms gliding around her to hold her close, so that she was totally wrapped in his embrace. In that instant everything went out of her head. She forgot all about time and place, and all she was aware of was the feel of him, the strength of his arms around her and the warmth that emanated from his body.

He kissed her lightly on each cheek, and Amber felt her pulse quicken and realised that her heart had begun to pump for all it was worth. A surge of heat ran through her from head to toe, and when he finally released her, she felt sure that her face must be filled with hot colour.

'No wonder my uncle was reluctant to part company with you.' He said the words in a soft undertone, and Amber felt the skin at the nape of her neck begin to prickle.

He didn't let her go entirely, though, even then. His hand remained, palm flat against the small of her back, and while she was glad at that moment of its steadying support, she was also conscious of the heat from those long fingers spreading like wildfire through her veins.

Ethan was more than just a mere man, she discovered. He was a tower of strength and authority, his every look and gesture shot through with a thread of steel that left no one in any doubt as to who was in command. And through it all he exuded the smouldering charisma of a red-blooded male intent on stalking his prey.

Amber had the distinct feeling that she was the one in his sights. She hadn't expected him to welcome her in such a way, or even at all, and she couldn't help wondering if this was a tactical manoeuvre. Perhaps he had decided that if there was no way of stopping her from coming here, he would watch her every move and bide his time.

'Shall we go?' he said, finally releasing her and taking hold of the wheelchair handles. Amber took the opportunity to gulp air into her lungs. 'We have a thirty-mile drive ahead of us, but I thought we might stop on the way for something to eat and drink.' He glanced at his uncle for confirmation. 'It's up to you, Martyn. It depends whether or not you want to go straight home. I know you've had a very long flight, and you've probably eaten on the plane.'

'We did,' Martyn said, 'though airline food is never completely satisfactory, is it?'

'That's true.' Ethan handed him the canvas bag. 'There are cool drinks in there. I thought you might need something to perk you up.'

'Thanks. Actually, I think a short stop along the

way might be a very good idea. I expect Amber might appreciate the chance to see something of our island, and maybe stretch her legs for a while.' Martyn looked at her to see what she thought of that idea, and Amber nodded.

'The island is beautiful,' she said. 'Just seeing it from the plane was enough to make me want to explore further.'

'We'll make a stop about halfway, then,' Ethan said. 'The road follows the coast for some distance, so you'll be able to look out and see the beaches and harbours along the way. If you look to your right, as we set off along the road, you'll see the mountains. The range stretches along almost the whole of the windward side of the island.'

He led them to his car. It was a gleaming silver saloon, beautifully upholstered inside and air-conditioned, so that the ride was wonderfully smooth and comfortable. Amber sat beside Ethan in the front of the car, giving Martyn more space in the back so that he could relax.

Ethan glanced at her from time to time, making light conversation and telling her about various landmarks along the way, while Martyn was content to doze some more. The road hugged the coastline for a while and beyond the built-up areas Amber caught glimpses of curving bays and rocky shores. As they left the coast behind and travelled northwards through the interior of the island, Ethan pointed out the volcanic mountain ranges on either side.

'That's the Waianae Range to the west,' he said. 'Just now we're passing through the central valley that divides those mountains from the Koolau Range.'

The scenery was breathtaking. She saw lush, tree-covered slopes, carpeted with ferns and decorated with the occasional outcrop of white blackberry flowers. Here and there she caught glimpses of water tumbling down a rock face or rivers winding their way through the valleys.

Up ahead, as they passed through a small township, she saw lakes on either side. 'In a few minutes we'll be driving by the plantation,' he said. 'We won't stop there today, because I think it might be too much for my uncle to cope with. I'll take you to look around it another day, if you like, when you're both rested and we have more time.'

Ethan glanced in the mirror at his sleeping uncle. 'He looks better than he did,' he murmured with a slight nod towards the back seat, 'but I suspect he's going to struggle much more than he had bargained for. This illness has taken its toll on him, hasn't it?'

'I'm afraid so.' She kept her voice low. 'Whatever the infection was that cut him down, it left a legacy that has permanently damaged his heart. He'll need to be very careful, whatever he does...and that means he should be shielded from any kind of stress. I think you should ask him to steer clear of getting involved with the plantation and any problems that crop up.'

'That's like asking a bubbling volcano to keep the pressure down,' Ethan said with a smile. 'You know what he's like. *Caution* isn't in his vocabulary.'

'Yes, I know. But I'm serious about this. No matter what we do with medication, it will only ever be palliative. As a doctor yourself, you must know that. We can improve his quality of life, but there's nothing more we can do to repair the damage, either surgically or with different drugs.'

He shot her a quick look. 'Knowing that, why did you choose to come with him? There isn't much that you'll be able to do to help him, is there?'

Her gaze meshed with his. 'I came because he asked me to, and because I've grown to care for him a lot over these last few weeks. He said he would feel better if he knew that I was with him. He trusts me, and he has confidence in me.'

'Isn't that misplaced confidence if you've admitted you can't do any more for him?'

'I don't think so. I've been upfront with him, and he's under no illusion about his limitations. It's more to do with peace of mind than anything else. He said he wanted to have me close by. He felt that you had enough on your plate with your work and the plantation, and he didn't want to be fussed over by strangers, by doctors he didn't know.'

'Hmm.' His gaze flicked over her. 'I can't help feeling there's more to it than that, but we'll see. He always was one to play his cards close to his chest.'

Amber frowned. She'd been as honest as she could, and yet she had the strong impression that he still suspected her motives…or maybe he thought his uncle was the one with a hidden agenda. Surely she knew his uncle better than that?

'We'll make a stop at a restaurant just up ahead,' Ethan murmured, changing the subject. 'Do you like chicken?'

'I do.'

'That's good. Among other things, they serve mouth-watering chicken dishes with rice, and delicious pancakes topped with ice cream and fruit for dessert. And they make a great mai tai, as well.'

'I've never had one of those.' She sent him a quick glance. 'What's a mai tai?'

His brows rose. 'You don't know? Oh, then you're in for a treat.' His smile lit up his features and watching the way his mouth curved in a crooked fashion caused Amber to catch her breath. There was no doubting that he was an extremely good-looking man. No wonder the girls didn't want to leave him alone. He made Amber's knees go weak, and she had thought she was immune.

'They're a mix of dark rum, light rum and orange curacao,' he explained, 'with a generous slosh of orange and lime juice, syrup and grenadine, all poured over shaved ice. There's a dash of orgeat in there, as well, a type of syrup made from almonds, sugar and rosewater. If you're lucky, it'll be garnished with a slice of pineapple and a cherry.'

'That sounds like a drink and a half.' She managed to stop herself from running her tongue over her lips in anticipation, but he must have guessed her impulse because he gave a soft laugh. 'It looks as though I've tempted you,' he murmured, a glimmer in his blue eyes.

He had the ways of the devil, she decided. He had a hot-blooded, take-charge manner and she had the feeling he would do his utmost to work his fiendish magic on her so that before too long she wouldn't know whether she was coming or going.

'You're right,' she said. 'I'm so thirsty I can

almost taste it. It must be the mere thought of relaxing in the heat of the day that's made me feel that way.' She would never admit that thoughts of having him sweep her into his arms had stirred her blood and caused all manner of wild imaginings to jump inside her head. Simply being in the car with him was enough for her to handle right now.

Martyn woke up as Ethan drew the car into the parking lot at the restaurant. 'Excellent,' he said. 'This is the perfect place for Amber to get a taste of Hawaiian life. I couldn't have chosen better myself.'

He turned down the use of the wheelchair. 'I can walk the short distance to the restaurant,' he said. Ethan helped him from the car, steadying him as he set foot on firm ground.

'Just smell that lovely fresh air.' Martyn looked about him and gave a beaming smile. 'Life is so good, isn't it?'

'It can be,' Ethan answered, glancing towards Amber.

She didn't know what was going through his

mind, but she decided to push any doubts into the background and concentrate instead on enjoying the spectacular surroundings. It seemed to Amber that there was colour in everything, beautiful bright splashes of green in the palms that decorated the forecourt and gardens of the restaurant, with brilliant sunspots of scarlet hibiscus and bright yellow bromeliads in the shrubbery.

They ate at a table outside, and as Amber sipped her mai tai and gazed around at the vista of hills and valleys all around, she reflected that just a few weeks ago she would never have envisaged that she would be sitting here in paradise. It would have been truly perfect except for the one flaw that she found hard to push to the back of her mind…the fact that Ethan was there. She was conscious of his brooding gaze resting on her in quiet, unguarded moments, and she had no way of knowing what he was thinking.

'If you're both finished, perhaps we should move on,' he said some time later. 'I expect you would both like to get home and settle in. We're coming to the end of a long day.' He looked at

Amber. 'You probably want to unpack and get used to your new surroundings.'

'Yes,' Amber said, 'That would be good.'

'Originally I was going to suggest that you stay up at the house with me,' Martyn said, 'but it's probably better this way. You'll have some privacy.'

'As I understand it, the bungalow is close by the house, so I'll be able to drop in on you easily enough if you need me.'

'That's right,' Martyn agreed. 'Ethan pointed out to me that the bungalow was empty, and it's still within the grounds of the main property, so it will be ideal.'

'But you must let me know any time if there's a problem, or you want help of any kind,' Amber said. 'That's what I'm here for, to take care of you.'

'I'm sure it will all work out very well.' He smiled. 'Anyway, Caitlin will be in the house with me when she comes home, and in the meantime Molly will be on hand to help out if I'm stuck.' He glanced at Amber. 'Molly is my housekeeper,' he added. 'I didn't want you to feel that you have to be at my beck and call all the time. It's just reassuring for me to know that you will be around, and perhaps you'll be able to keep me company some evenings.'

'Of course.' Amber sent Ethan a quick look. 'I suggested that we set up a pager system so that I can go to him right away if he needs me,' she said. 'You should be on the link, too.'

He nodded. 'I'm with you on that one. I've already set the wheels in motion.'

He helped his uncle back to the car and saw him settled comfortably. Watching them, Amber couldn't help thinking that their relationship was more like that of father and son. She could see the affection in Martyn's eyes when he looked at Ethan, and she knew from the gentle and considerate way that Ethan attended to his uncle that the feeling was mutual.

The journey to Martyn's house didn't take more than half an hour. Dusk was closing in when Ethan finally pulled into the driveway, and Amber was immediately impressed by the beautiful villa that Martyn called home.

It was a two-storey house, colour washed to a

pale sand finish, with sloping roofs at different levels, while the veranda was made up of white-painted hardwood decking.

'Now, this I recognise,' Amber said with a smile, looking at Ethan. 'It's where you stood when you made the video link.'

He nodded. 'And if you go just around the corner you'll see the bay in all its glory.'

'I can already hear the sound of the sea,' she murmured, tilting her head so that the faint breeze caught her hair and lifted the soft tendrils. 'I can smell it on the air, too. It's lovely.'

'You have a beautiful home,' she said, turning to Martyn. 'Let me help you inside. You look weary.'

'I am, but I'm happier than I've been in a long time.' He glanced at Ethan. 'It was good of you to take time out to come and fetch us. I know how busy you are. If you want to drop my cases off, I think I'll go straight up to my room.'

'Of course. I'll help you.'

Martyn shook his head. 'It's all right. Molly and Ben are here. They'll see to everything. You take Amber along to her place and make sure that she settles in all right.'

Molly opened the door and greeted him with an expansive smile. 'Oh, it's good to have you back,' she said. She was a woman of around fifty years of age, Amber guessed. She had the honey-bronzed skin of a native Hawaiian, and she introduced the man alongside her as Ben, her husband.

'You leave everything to us,' Molly reassured Martyn. 'Ben will take your cases upstairs and unpack for you, and I'll lay out your things ready for bed.'

Martyn greeted both of them in turn, and then he turned to Amber and gave her a hug. 'You should have everything you need at the bungalow. If there's anything missing, just let Ethan know, and he'll put it right. If you don't mind, I'll show you around in the morning. I think I've had enough excitement for one day.'

She returned the embrace. 'Of course I don't mind. That will be great. You go and get some rest and I'll see you tomorrow.'

He nodded. 'Come and have breakfast with me.'

'I'll do that.'

The bungalow was just a short walk along a winding path through overhanging trees and shrubs. Martyn showed her the way, helping her with her cases, and waiting while she put the key into the lock. It was a neat house, white painted, with soft green wooden shutters at the windows and the all-important veranda going all the way round the building.

'You'll be able to sit out on the sundeck,' Ethan said. 'From the back of the house you can look out over the seashore. It's really beautiful first thing in the morning.'

He carried her bags inside. 'You want these put anywhere in particular?' he asked. 'The bedroom is through there.'

'That will do fine,' she murmured. She peered in through the doorway and saw a pastel-coloured room with pale carpets and filmy drapes at the windows. The bed was large, covered with a beautiful, floral-print duvet that picked out the colours in the drapes and in various ornaments around the room. There was a built-in dressing table and several glass-fronted wardrobes with drapes that matched the window curtains. In all, it was a beautiful room.

'You have your own sitting-room through there,' Ethan pointed out, dropping off the cases and showing her into a light, airy living space with glass doors opening out onto a terrace. 'There is your sea view,' he said indicating the area beyond the doors.

Amber gave a soft gasp. 'It's incredible,' she said softly. 'I think I must have died and gone to heaven.' Through the doors, she could see the vast sweep of a bay, with rocky promontories pushing out into the ocean, and as the sun was setting the sky was lit with orange flame, throwing up silhouettes of the coconut palms and broad-leaved ironwood trees that grew along the shore. Close by the doors was a mango tree, heavy with fruit that were beginning to turn from yellow to red. All she had to do was reach out and pick one.

'I knew I would find everything so different out here, but I don't think I ever imagined it would be as lovely as this…right on my doorstep.'

He gave a faint smile. 'I suppose we get used to it, living here. Perhaps we take it for granted.' He turned around to look at the room. 'Do you think you'll be okay here? You have a writing desk, TV and music centre, and of course there's a computer.'

She was nodding, still too bemused to answer properly. The furnishings were beautifully upholstered in soft, warm colours that were easy on the eye. 'I can't think of anything else I could possibly need.'

He started to walk towards the door. 'That's good. Through here is your kitchen. It's not tremendously big, but there's enough room for a small table and chairs, and of course you have a cooker and a microwave. The fridge has been stocked for you, along with the freezer, but if there's anything you're short of, I can fix that for you. I'm only next door, so you only have to give me a shout.'

'Next door? You mean, up at the house?'

He shook his head. 'I was staying there temporarily while Martyn was in the U.K. I have my own place further along the coast, but since I'm spending more time at the plantation these days, it's easier for me to live here. My bungalow is right next to this one. If you look out of the kitchen window, you'll see my back door.'

Amber glanced about the kitchen while she tried to take that in. It gave her time to think, and to adjust to what he was saying.

The units were made of wood, finished in a soft apple-green colour, so pale as to be restful on the eyes, with some of them glass fronted, and there were lots of shelving units and bottle racks, along with all the modern fittings anyone could want.

She glanced through the window. The back of his bungalow was just a few paces away, as he had said. From here, she would be able to see him sitting out on his veranda whenever he decided to take the air, and the same would go for him.

'I hadn't realised you would be my neighbour,' she said. 'Well, I thought you might be up at the house from time to time, but Martyn told me you had your own place a few miles away.'

He smiled, coming over to her and sliding an

arm about her shoulders. 'Did you really think I would stay away and leave you to your own devices?' His fingers trailed through the silky hair at her nape. 'That was never going to happen.'

His long body was close to hers, so close that she could feel the beat of his heart against her breast. It thumped out a steady rhythm, a relentless drumbeat that let her know he was in control, he was watching her, and he had everything worked out.

'You don't trust me at all, do you?' she murmured.

'Not a centimetre,' he answered softly. 'Not even a hair's breadth.' His head lowered, so that his cheek was close to hers, his lips just a breath away. 'I can see very well why my uncle is so taken with you. You're everything a man could want, and I'd be a liar if I said I was immune to your charms. But just so that you know, I'll be close by. I'll be watching everything you do, every move you make.'

He dropped a kiss lightly on her mouth, a touch that was feather-like and as insubstantial as thistledown, and yet the imprint of that kiss stayed with her long after he was gone. She felt the burning embers of it as though he had branded her with flame. It was a kiss that said, Beware, be careful what you do, because I may show you the consequences of any action you take.

CHAPTER SIX

AMBER stared, bleary-eyed, at herself in the mirror in the bathroom. How could she have slept for so long? No sooner had her head touched the pillow than she had fallen into a deep, deep sleep, and yet she didn't feel refreshed. She felt a little odd.

Perhaps was still suffering from jet-lag. It had certainly been the longest journey she had ever undertaken, enough to put the strongest person out of synch. Somehow, though, she had the notion there was more to it than that.

This was to all intents and purposes the beginning of a new phase in her life. She had come all this way to start afresh. Wasn't that the reason she was here? Yes, Martyn had said he wanted her help and she had agreed to stay with him through these difficult months of recovery, but if she was honest with herself, hadn't she also been running away from the situation back home?

In truth, the thought of James getting closer to Caitlin day by day had been more than she could bear, and maybe Ethan was right to suspect her motives in coming here. Wasn't she doing this job under false pretences? What made her think she could make any difference in Martyn's life? Shouldn't she have stayed at home and tried to make the best of things? Some kind of work would have come along eventually, wouldn't it? But instead of waiting to see what might happen, she had taken the coward's way out.

She stepped under the shower and hoped that the warm spray of water would gradually wash away her doubts. Perhaps it was strange that she was feeling this way, when she ought to be overwhelmed with happiness at finding herself in an idyllic tropical paradise, but Ethan's warning was running persistently through her head, and it had played like a haunting refrain throughout her dreams last night.

She stepped out of the shower a few minutes later, wrapping a towelling robe around herself before going into the bedroom to dry her hair.

She switched off the hairdrier after a few minutes and heard a faint knocking sound coming from the front of the house. 'Amber, are you there? Are you awake?' She set the drier down on the dressing table and became aware of Ethan's voice, threaded through with a faint note of frustration. How long had he been knocking?

Pulling the robe more closely around her and securing the belt, she hurried to answer the door. 'I'm sorry,' she said, stepping back a little and inviting him in with a small wave of her hand. 'I didn't hear you above the noise of the hairdrier. Have you been waiting long?'

'A few minutes. It doesn't matter.' He looked her over from head to toe, an appreciative glint coming into his blue eyes as he surveyed the creamy expanse of her shoulder where the robe had slipped a little, and then his gaze moved to trail along the length of her smooth, lightly tanned legs. Instinctively, she drew the lapels of the robe together.

'I realise time's getting on,' she said. 'I must have slept through the alarm, but I was hoping I'd still make it in time to have breakfast with Martyn. He said the meal would be later than usual.' Then she frowned as another thought struck her. 'Is he all right? I rang the house last night and gave Molly the instructions for his medication.'

'He's fine, don't worry about it. He's suffering a bit from the effects of all the travelling, and asked me to tell you that breakfast will be delayed even further. I'd have left you alone, but it occurred to me that you might not find your way about too easily. There are footpaths going off in all directions around here, some leading to the beach, others to the coastal path. It's easy to be confused with all the trees and greenery obscuring the view.'

He walked through to the kitchen. 'Since I'm here, shall I make some coffee? You look as though you could do with a cup of something. Adorable as you look with that confused, sleepy expression, I think you'd appreciate being wide-awake for a tour around the place. We could take a walk down to the beach while we're waiting for Molly to cook breakfast, if you like?'

'That sounds like a good idea.' It was almost like being on holiday. Having someone take over the running of the household and see to all the catering was way beyond her experience. Ethan lived in a completely different world from her. 'Does she always make breakfast for you?'

'Whenever I'm around, or when Martyn is home…along with lunch, dinner, supper or whatever takes her fancy. Molly's a great person to have around. Her husband, Ben, does all the odd jobs around the place, and keeps the grounds in order.'

'Wow. How the other half live.' She smiled. 'I'm impressed…and coffee would be lovely, thanks. I haven't figured out yet how to use the grinder, so I made do with juice last night. It was delicious, though, like nothing I've ever tasted before.'

'That would be the produce from our plantation,' he murmured. 'It's fresh as can be, so I'm glad you like it.' He walked over to a cupboard and took out a bag of coffee beans. 'We grow this on our land, too, but we don't export it in large quantities. The locals really like it, and it's an indulgence I look forward to every day. It keeps me awake when I have a long day at the hospital. Come over here and let me show you how to work the machine.'

Amber did as he asked, and he began to assemble the various parts of the apparatus. 'You fit the blades in here, see, and then set it on the stand, like so… It can be a bit tricky… Here, you come and try for yourself.'

She gave it her best effort, but the whole thing was seated wrongly and he reached around her to give the base a twist. 'It's a bit awkward if you don't know how. It's a new gadget, one of those "do everything except wash the dishes" types… It doubles up as a food mixer, blender, grinder. That's why there are so many parts to it.'

She felt his arms go around her and he took her

hand and showed her how the mechanism worked. She felt the heat rise in her as his body moved closer to hers. His thigh was touching hers, his chest was nudging the length of her back, and his arms were closing in on her like an embrace.

'The whole thing was disassembled while no one was living here,' he said. 'This bit plugs into the mains electricity. And now you just tip in a few beans, see, like this?'

'Yes, I see,' she managed. It was hard to think straight with him holding her that way. 'It was just that I didn't know how to put it all together, but it's clear now that you've shown me.' Now that the gadget was assembled, the rest was plain sailing, but he hadn't stepped back from her, and she was altogether too conscious of his nearness. She could feel the warmth of his body through the towelling robe, and he was close enough that she registered the restrained power locked in his broad shoulders.

She added the coffee beans.

'That's good. Now fix the top cover in place, switch on, and away you go.'

She followed his instructions and the aroma of freshly ground coffee filled the air. He breathed it in, and bent his head towards her so that she felt the faintly roughened texture of his face against hers. 'Isn't that something special? The test will be in the final brew, of course.'

'I… Yes…' she said huskily. 'Um…perhaps I should go and get dressed. I wouldn't want to keep Martyn waiting for too long.'

A glimmer of amusement crossed his face, and she realised that he had known full well what he was doing, all along, and he was well aware of how flustered she had become. Right now he had the upper hand, and it was disconcerting to know that he would exert his control over her at any opportunity.

He eased back from her, and she fled to the bedroom, her heart beating out a frantic rhythm and her cheeks flushed with soft colour.

The coffee was steaming gently in the perco-lator when she returned to the kitchen. By now she was much more composed, and it helped that she was wearing clothes that were much less controversial, a T-shirt and white trousers, and her hair was tied back in a more orderly fashion, so that only a few tendrils escaped to trail along her cheeks.

He handed her a mug of the hot liquid, and she added cream and sugar before sipping the contents. 'Mmm…it tastes like a small piece of heaven,' she murmured. She had herself under control now, and Ethan could do his worst. She wouldn't rise to his bait.

Perhaps he sensed the change in her, because he let go of the playful mood and concentrated on finding out if everything in the house was to her satisfaction.

'It's more than perfect,' she said. 'I hadn't expected any of this. It's like a home from home—more so, in fact. I could never have aspired to anything like this. When Martyn first put forward the possibility of me coming out here, I thought I would have a room in the main house, perhaps, or at the most, a small flat. After all, my job was to come out here and keep an eye on your uncle, and make sure that his medication was appropriate…but, of course, that doesn't involve very much. We might need to vary the dosage from week to week to ensure that his heart pumps adequately, but otherwise things should run pretty smoothly.'

'But you do know that he's very fond of you? That can't have escaped you. He was determined to keep you close at hand.'

'It's a mutual feeling.' She sent him a quick look. 'I know you think there's more to it, but I like your uncle very much. I took to him right away. I believe he asked me to come here because he wants the reassurance of a friendly face close by. As a doctor, you must know yourself that when someone has been near to death they become apprehensive about the future. Caitlin is busy with her own life, which is only natural because she's young and on the threshold of everything, and Martyn is too generous a man to expect her to come home with him and take care of him.'

'My uncle has never been short of company or lacked friends about him. Come to that, he has Molly and Ben with him the whole time. They live in at the house.' Ethan returned her gaze with a penetrating stare. 'There's more going on here than my uncle is letting on. He is a very wealthy man, and he is used to having things his own way. Maybe you don't know any more about it than I do, but all I can say is that I will protect him in any way I can. He's more than an uncle to me. He's been like a father, and I won't stand by and see him hurt in any way.'

'And it's right that you should do that.' She tilted her head to one side, giving him a questioning look. 'Perhaps we could call a truce…at least we could put up a united front to help him get through these next few months with as little stress as possible.'

'A truce?' He came over to her and lifted her hand, placing it between his palms. His grasp was light but firm, and having him hold her that way sent a strange thrill of excitement coursing through her body. He raised her hand and held it to his lips, brushing softly over the smoothness of her skin. 'A truce, sealed with a kiss. Now, that's something that should stand the test of time.'

He looked at her, his gaze brooding, the pressure on her hand increasing momentarily, and then he relinquished his grasp on her and she felt a sense of confusion, as though something momentous had happened, but she couldn't quite fathom what it was.

'Let's go for a short walk along the bay,' he said after a minute or two. 'You can tell me a little about the job my uncle found for you at the hospital. I expect you'd like to go and look around there some time before you start, and maybe see something of the town. We can arrange all that over the next day or so. You start work there in a couple of weeks, don't you?'

'That's right.'

They set off to walk along the sand just a short time later, and Amber stopped every now and again to gather up shells that had been washed ashore by the incoming tide.

'It's a surfers' paradise along this part of the coast,' Ethan told her. 'The ocean is calm now, but in winter the waves are higher than any you'll ever see.'

Amber looked out over the ocean, shielding her eyes from the glare of the sun. 'What's that I can see in the water?' she asked. 'I can't quite make them out.'

'They're green turtles,' he told her. 'They nest further along the coast, and sometimes they come up on the beach. Occasionally, you'll see whales or dolphins out at sea.'

They watched the turtles for a while, and then Amber went on with her search for shells. She had taken off her sandals and was walking barefoot across the warm, wet sand at the water's edge. Ethan pointed out white-breasted sanderlings hopping to and fro, searching for small crustaceans or insect larvae that might dwell among the damp grains of sand, all the while deftly avoiding the incoming waves.

There were turnstones, too, searching for any tasty morsels that might be lurking under rocks and seaweed. Every now and then they would take flight, moving their prized finds out of reach of other birds.

After a while, Ethan suggested that it was time

they set off for the house. 'Molly will be waiting for us,' he said. 'She was planning on giving us quite a feast, though I doubt Martyn will manage very much of it. He wasn't eating too well in hospital, was he?'

'He'll have to take things gradually, and with any luck his appetite will improve.'

She had certainly worked up an appetite herself by now, and her earlier sleepiness had dissolved, blown away by the faint breeze and the exhilaration of walking along this beautiful bay. The fact that Ethan had made it his business to charm her along the way had probably helped.

Molly had been true to her word, Amber discovered as Martyn showed her into the dining-room just off the main kitchen. The table had been laid with a variety of colourful dishes to tempt the palate, along with a coffee pot, cream and sugar and jugs filled with freshly squeezed juice.

'I hope you settled in all right last night,' Martyn said. 'I'm sorry I couldn't show you around the house, but tiredness suddenly swept over me.'

'I'm amazed you coped as well as you did,'

Amber told him. 'I thought the idea was that you should take things easy, so you did exactly the right thing in going to bed.'

'Well, I had a wonderful night's sleep. Come and sample some of Molly's glorious food. Ethan, you sit yourself down opposite Amber, and both of you eat up. I really want you to enjoy this breakfast. It's a special occasion with all of us together this way.'

Ethan sat down by Martyn's right-hand side. 'You should try these delicious Hawaiian wraps,' he told Amber. 'You can make them yourself in a matter of minutes, and they're a wonderful start to the day.'

Each wrap consisted of a tortilla filled with egg that had been scrambled and mixed with lightly browned chopped ham and red and green peppers. There was a hint of pineapple in there, too, and the wraps were served with wedges of watermelon.

'You're right,' Amber agreed, adding one to her plate and taking a bite. She savoured the mouth-watering flavours. 'What a lovely way to begin the day.'

'Molly's made my favourite, the Hawaiian royal,' Martyn said. 'It's made with Portuguese spicy sausage, green onions and eggs over a bed of rice. If you add a touch of mustard to the dish, it's absolutely out of this world.'

He helped himself to the food, but Amber noticed he only ate a very small amount. He looked better than he had done in a long while, but she knew that he had to be careful.

'I hope you're going to sit back and relax now that you're home,' Amber said, giving him a quick glance.

'Certainly, I am,' he murmured. 'I had it in mind that, since Ethan isn't working today, he could show you around, maybe even take you into town to look over the hospital where you'll be working. It's entirely up to you, of course. You might prefer simply to spend some time on the beach.'

'We've already been down there this morning,' she told him. 'It was a wonderful experience.'

Martyn looked pleased. 'That's good.' He dabbed his mouth on a serviette and then put the linen to one side. 'I thought I would go and spend some time in my study,' he said. 'I want to reacquaint myself with a few things.'

'You mean, you're going to be looking over the plantation records, don't you?' Ethan said, giving him a stern look. 'Do you really think that's a good idea?'

'Absolutely, I do,' Martyn said with a smile. 'I can't think of any better way to spend my time. I love that plantation. It's been my life's work.' He pushed back his chair and carefully stood up. 'Forgive me if I leave you two together for a while,' he said.

He put out a hand to stop her when Amber would have stood up and gone with him to see him out of the room. 'I can manage,' he said, 'and if I have any problems later, I know how to get in touch with you.' He indicated the pager that was clipped to his belt. 'I don't anticipate any trouble, and I have Molly and Ben to look out for me. You should concentrate on settling in and getting used to your surroundings. Perhaps I'll see you later this afternoon?'

'Of course, if you're sure you'll be all right?' Amber sent him a doubtful look.

'I'll be fine.'

Martyn left the room, and Ethan commented softly, 'He's a strong-willed man, and it doesn't do any good to try to oppose him, once he's made up his mind. He knows what he wants, and sometimes it's less wearing on him and everyone else to let him have his way…or at least to let him think he has what he wants.' He gave Amber a thoughtful look. 'So, what would you like to do today? I could take you to see the sights, or perhaps you'd like to do some shopping in town?'

'Actually, I think I'd quite like to see the plantation, if that wouldn't be too much trouble.'

His eyes narrowed on her, and she wondered if he was debating with himself why she would want to see the source of the family's wealth, so she hurried to explain, 'I've heard so much about it, and it seems to be very dear to Martyn's heart. Perhaps once I've seen it, I'll understand more.'

'That would be no trouble at all. It's just a short drive away from here. In fact, now I come to think of it, I believe there will be a *luau* later on today, to be held on one of the beaches nearby. It's one of the events staged by the company, and the proceeds will go to local charities. It will go on late into the evening, and I think it's something you might enjoy.'

'That sounds good to me,' she said brightly, but then she frowned. 'Your uncle asked if I would spend some time with him this evening. Is it something that he would enjoy?'

'I'm sure he will, though I doubt he'll want to stay to the end. I'll let him know what we're planning.'

With that decided, they spent the rest of the morning and part of the afternoon wandering around the plantation. Amber was amazed by the sheer size of it, and she was impressed by the colour and beauty of everything around her. There were hundreds of plants and trees of many varieties, and it was clear that these were of interest to visitors of all ages. She saw lots of children excitedly rushing about while their parents tried valiantly to keep up with them.

'We don't just specialise in pineapples,' Ethan told her. 'As I said, we grow coffee, along with cacao, bananas, papayas and mangos.'

'It looks as though you grow flowers, as well,' Amber said, her eyes widening as she tried to take in everything about her. 'I've never seen so many varieties, and such beauty.'

'The hibiscus is native to Hawaii,' he explained, 'but we grow flowers for the traditional leis, the garlands that people wear around their necks, as well.'

Amber was overwhelmed by the scale of everything. 'I had never imagined it would be as vast as this,' she murmured. Just to get around the place, they'd had to use a motorised cart. 'No wonder Martyn worries about it. It's such a responsibility.'

'We employ a lot of people,' Ethan said. 'I suppose the key to good management is to delegate. It's something Martyn's going to have to learn to do.'

It was mid-afternoon when they returned to the house. Amber discovered Martyn sitting out on the veranda, taking the air, so she went and sat beside him and told him all about the tour. He seemed pleased that she appreciated the extent of his life's work.

Amber chatted with him for a while and made sure that he was feeling as well as he said he did. She took his blood pressure and checked his pulse, and then looked at his tablet dispenser to see if he had taken his medication on time.

'*Aloha auina la…*good afternoon,' Molly said, coming out onto the veranda with a tray of cold drinks. She placed it down on a table. 'I hope you had a good day with Mr Ethan,' she added, looking at Amber. 'You don't need to worry about Mr Martyn. I took good care of him. I made certain that he took his tablets at the right time.'

'Thank you for that, Molly,' Amber said with a smile. 'I felt sure that I could rely on you to remind him.' She looked at the tray that Molly had set down. 'These drinks look delicious.' There were jugs of various kinds of fruit juices, decorated with slices of pineapple, cherries and limes.

Molly returned the smile. 'Enjoy,' she said, leaving them and going back into the house.

Amber turned back to Martyn. 'So, do you feel rested?' she asked him. 'Will you come with us to the *luau* later on?'

He nodded. 'Yes. I'd like that. I'm glad that Ethan mentioned it to you. It will be a good way for you to celebrate the beginning of your time here.'

Amber sat with him for a while longer, until he looked at the watch on his wrist and suggested that it was time to start getting ready for the *luau*. 'Ethan said he would come and pick us up at six, so perhaps we should prepare for the evening.'

Molly appeared out of nowhere and began to help him to his feet. 'Do you want Ben to give you a hand?' she asked. 'He's finished clearing the weeds out of the vegetable garden, so he's got nothing at all to do right now.'

Amber didn't hear his muffled reply. As the hours wore on, she was becoming more and more doubtful about why she was actually there. Martyn didn't need her, that was for sure. He had ample help already.

It didn't take her long to get ready for the party. She changed into a simple shift dress that clung softly to her curves. It would be cool enough to counteract the heat of the evening, and yet it was dressy enough for the occasion. She let her hair hang loose about her shoulders and added a dab of lipstick to the generous curve of her lips.

By the time Ethan called for them, she was up at the house, ready to help Martyn into the car.

The beach where the party was taking place was just a few minutes' drive away. Ethan parked in the shade of trees, and then took Martyn's arm and helped him to a seating area set back a little from the water's edge. Amber went to join him at the table, her senses taken up with the sights and sounds all around her.

Hawaiian music was playing in the background, and girls dressed in traditional costume, wearing leis around their shoulders and flowers in their hair, were dancing barefoot just a short distance away. The scent of roast pork came from a barbecue stand just to the back of her, and all the tables were set with platters of fruit, a variety of salads, along with bowls of chicken, rice and sweet potatoes.

Amber leaned towards Martyn. 'If you keep spoiling me with treats like this, I'll never want to go home.'

Martyn gave a soft laugh and squeezed her hand. 'I'm really glad that you like it here. Relax and enjoy yourself.'

'I thought you might like to try some of our island cocktails,' Ethan said, coming towards them with a tray of drinks. He glanced from one to the other, and Amber knew that he had witnessed the gentle show of affection between herself and his uncle. She tried not to let it bother her. Ethan could think what he liked. She wasn't going to let him put her on the defensive all the time.

'Perhaps we should drink to King Kamehameha,' Ethan said, pushing a long glass of something golden towards Martyn and handing her a cocktail glass filled with a bright red concoction and decorated with fruit and a sparkler that fizzed coloured light in all directions. He raised his own glass and then sipped slowly from it.

'King Kamehameha? I don't think I know anything about him.'

'He was a king who founded a dynasty out here. It's said that when he was born his grandfather was warned that he would slay the chiefs and usurp his position when he grew up, so his grandfather ordered that he should be killed.'

Amber stared at him in horror. 'Tell me that didn't happen.'

'It didn't happen.' Ethan smiled. 'Instead, the child was hidden away and brought up by a childless couple, who kept him safe. Then, five years later, his grandfather discovered that he was alive. He was full of remorse for what he had tried to do, and so the boy was allowed to return to court, where he was taught the ways of court diplomacy and served as a loyal aide to his uncle. After that, he became a successful warrior and fought wars to unify Hawaii. I suppose the slaying of chiefs was to do with enemies rather than any family hostilities.'

'And so now we celebrate with feasting and music,' Martyn said.

Just then there was a blaze of light all around as torches were lit and someone began to blow into a conch shell. An expectant hush descended on the gathered crowd.

'What's happening? What does it mean?' Amber asked in a whisper.

'The royal court is arriving by boat,' Ethan told her. 'It's all symbolic. The fire dancers will signify the battles that were fought, and after that it will be time for celebrating. There will be dancing and feasting and generally making merry.'

It was all good fun, and as darkness fell the entertainment began in earnest. Amber's eyes widened as the fire dancers swooped and swirled and flirted with danger.

'You look as though you're enjoying yourself,' Martyn said softly. 'I'm glad about that. It's good to see a sparkle in your eyes.' He looked around and saw that Ben was coming towards him. 'I'm going to let Ben take me home now,' he added, and when Amber would have stood up to leave with him he shook his head and laid a hand on her shoulder. 'You stay and have a good time,' he murmured. 'I expect Ethan will dance with you and show you how we celebrate our good fortune out here. I'll see you in the morning.'

She watched him go, a slight frown gathering on her forehead, and then Ethan was urging her to go and dance with him, just as Martyn had said. He reached for her, clasping her hand and drawing her out on to the flat sand where people were swaying to the rhythm of the music.

His arms curved about her, and perhaps it was the intoxicating effect of the cocktails she had been drinking, but it seemed after that as though the world was made of pure sensation. She was aware of his hard body pressed against hers, the nudge of his leg against her thigh, the gentle glide of his hand over the small of her back, drawing her ever closer to him. And over all was a canopy of stars, sprinkled against the back-cloth of a midnight sky.

The haunting music lulled her senses, filling her being, and she and Ethan moved together in harmony with the gentle rhythm. It was perfect, sensual, a throbbing heartbeat of heavenly ex-perience, and even though she realised she had sipped just a little too much of the alcoholic drinks that Ethan had been bringing her throughout the evening, it was the fact that he was holding her that was making her feel this way.

Why did Ethan have this effect on her? She barely knew him. She had only met him a few weeks ago, and yet all her thoughts were taken up with him. As he lowered his head towards her, it seemed like the most natural thing in the world that he should kiss her. His lips descended, touched, tasted, settled, lingering to explore the sweet, curving line of her mouth.

Her whole body tingled with the exhilaration of that kiss. It spread through her like flame, burning like a fever. She kissed him in return, her lips clinging, tasting, savouring the feel of him, so that her whole world took on a golden, warm glow.

'You see,' Ethan murmured, reluctantly dragging his lips from hers, so that they could both come up for air, 'you and I could have it all. You fit so perfectly into my arms as though you were made for me alone. I could give you whatever it is that you want.'

He gazed down at her, his blue eyes glittering in the darkness. 'I'm here, now… I want you, and I know you feel the same way about me. I can feel it in the way your body quivers next to mine, in the way your lips soften when I kiss you. Isn't that the truth? Don't you feel it the same way I do, running through your veins like quicksilver?'

That was exactly how she felt. Her soft, feminine curves were crushed against him, and she wanted to be even closer, if that was possible, but the music was sounding a drumbeat in her head, and the thunder of her heart was overwhelming, setting off an alarm throughout her body.

She pressed a shaky hand against his chest. 'I don't know what I want,' she said raggedly. 'This is all happening so quickly. I only know it's too soon… It's this Hawaiian paradise weaving its spell on me. I've had too much to drink, and I'm not thinking straight.'

She tried to ease back from him, to allow a faint, cool breeze to clear her head, but he wasn't about to let her go.

His gaze meshed with hers. 'I have wealth and power, too…you can have whatever you want. You only have to say the word and it's yours.'

Amber was bewildered. 'I don't understand… Why would you say something like that?'

'You already know the answer to that one, don't you?' His hands caressed her, smoothing over the curve of her hips and lightly pressuring her towards him once again. 'I wanted you the first moment I saw you. You're so beautiful…you stir a man's blood until he doesn't know what he's doing any more.'

She started to shake her head. This sort of thing didn't happen to her. She was caught up in the island's spell, and her inhibitions had dissolved in the heat, and everything from then on had gone haywire.

'I can give you your heart's desire,' he said softly. 'You only have to say the word and it's yours. I owe you a debt for ever because you saved my uncle's life.'

She frowned, mist swirling inside her head. 'Is this all because of your uncle?'

'We can work this out between us.' Ethan's voice was soft, hypnotic. 'Are you so set on letting him lose his heart to you? He's not himself these days. All he can talk about is that he's found you and that he feels blessed because you agreed to come out here with him. What kind of hold do you have on him?'

'I don't have a hold on him.' She gazed at him in consternation. Surely he couldn't really believe what he was saying? 'This doesn't make any sense at all.'

'It all seems perfectly clear to me. He's ill and he's not thinking straight. You saved his life and he wants to repay you for that in some way, but he's taking things to the extreme, and you're going along with it, sucking him in deeper. Why don't you let me save you from yourself? He doesn't need to be hurt in any way. We can sort this out, you and me. You decide what it will take for you to leave him be.'

Amber stared up at him, letting his words flow over her until they began to rain down on her like a cold shower. Everything he had done, everything he had said had been a pretence, a mockery. He didn't care for her at all. He simply wanted to get her away from his uncle.

'How could you?' she asked. 'How could you say such things to me?'

She turned away from him and started to run along the path that led away from the beach. She would not listen to what he had to say. She ignored him when he called her name. All she knew was that she had to get away from him. She had to go back to her temporary home, and she would do it under her own steam. She wanted nothing more to do with him.

CHAPTER SEVEN

'WHAT'S going on with you and Mr Ethan? Have you and he had words?' Molly was preparing food in the kitchen, getting ready for an early breakfast. She was cooking omelettes, wonderful, fluffy creations that Amber knew from experience melted in the mouth, but now she paused, looking directly at Amber.

'What makes you say that?'

Molly gave her an old-fashioned look. 'You think I don't know about these things? Hah!' Molly shook her head and began to deftly slice peppers, wielding the knife like an expert before tossing the brightly coloured chunks into the pan with the eggs. 'It's going on too long. I see you, this last couple of weeks, avoiding looking at each other, not talking unless you have to.'

'Um…I suppose you could say we had a difference of opinion, if you like. But we're fine, really.' Amber sent Molly an anxious look. 'I was hoping it didn't show. Neither of us wants to upset Martyn in any way.'

'*Uwe!* I think he probably guessed already.' Molly gave the eggs a quick stir, then angled the spatula towards Amber, shaking it briefly, 'You think he doesn't know what's going on? You're wrong. That man knows everything.'

'Oh, dear.' Amber thought about that for a moment or two. 'But if he does know, it doesn't seem to bother him at all.'

Molly smiled. 'He's very wise. He knows these things have a way of working themselves out. Me? I think you need to sort it out.' She sniffed the air. 'The bagels are done…you want to fetch them out of the oven?'

'Yes, of course.' Amber picked up the oven gloves and slid the tray out, tipping the freshly baked bagels onto a warm platter. 'Will it be all right if I take one of these to go? I'm supposed to start work at the hospital this morning, and I want to be there early so that I have time to familiarise myself with everything. I've already spoken to Martyn about missing breakfast.'

'That's fine.' Molly indicated the array of fillings set out on the worktop. 'Help yourself to bacon and tomatoes. I made you some salad. You want to take that with you? It's in the fridge.'

Amber smiled and dropped a quick kiss on her cheek. 'You're an angel,' she said. 'I love you to bits.'

'Heh-heh. Me, too. You good for Mr Martyn. He's perked up no end since you've been around.' Molly tipped the omelettes on to a plate. 'You take care in this new job. Don't let them boss you around. You're just a slip of a girl, but you know what you doing.'

Amber grinned. She hoped Molly was right about that. A new job, a new hospital, different people to get to know…it all promised to be quite an experience.

She had bought herself a small car, refusing

Martyn's offer of help, and so the journey to the hospital was an easy one. She knew the route fairly well, since Ethan had shown her the way a few days ago. He had stayed with her while she'd looked around the place where she would be working and then he'd disappeared on an errand while she'd met the people who would be her colleagues.

Molly had clearly picked up on the atmosphere between the two of them. This last couple of weeks had been fraught with problems, since both she and Ethan had their own particular grievances and were thrown together daily in their contact with Martyn. It had been difficult being in the same room with Ethan, let alone having him as a neighbour, but they had come to an agreement of sorts. They had to be together for as long as she was in Hawaii, and so they would make the best of things, for Martyn's sake.

They both knew where they stood. Ethan didn't trust her and she was always guarded in her dealings with him.

She tried to put all that behind her as she drove

along the valley road. The lush, forested slopes had a soothing effect on her, so that by the time she arrived at the hospital she was on good form.

The hospital was a modern building in the middle of a thriving town. Surrounded by lakes and green hills, it was pleasing on the eye, a pleasant place to work. Her job here was to help out in Accident and Emergency, with an element of going out to treat patients outside of hospital, if necessary. As she understood things, she would be working alongside a consultant and senior house officers. Her immediate boss was a young Hawaiian doctor, a registrar named Kyle. She had met him on that first visit and he seemed friendly and confident about what he was doing. There was a monthly rota system in operation for callouts.

'How are you doing?' Kyle greeted her cheerily as she was trying to find her bearings.

'I'm all right, I think,' she said. 'I've said hello to all the doctors and nurses on duty, I know where the charts and the lab forms are stored, and I've discovered where all the equipment is kept. So I think I'm about ready to make a start.'

'That's great.' He handed her a chart. 'Your first patient shouldn't be too difficult to handle. She's a young girl who was walking on the beach when she felt something wrap itself around her foot. Then she was stung, but someone has already removed the spine that was stuck in her foot.'

'So what kind of creature stung her, do we know?' She glanced through the notes, but there was no answer in there.

'I'd guess a stingray,' Kyle said. 'They have an appendage that has sharp, sword-like stingers that can do some real damage. The stingers are filled with venom, so you have both a puncture wound and a poison to deal with.'

'Thanks for that,' Amber acknowledged him. 'I'll go and take a look at her.'

'Okay. Let me know if you have any problems.'

'I will.'

The girl was about fourteen years old, and she was clearly in a distressed state. She'd been vomiting, and appeared to be feeling faint.

'Hello, Lara,' Amber greeted her. 'I'm Dr Shaw. Let's see what needs to be done about your injury, shall we?' She smiled at the girl's mother, letting her explain what had happened.

A nurse had already cleaned the wound, and Lara was soaking her foot in water that was as hot as she could bear. The nurse frequently checked the temperature and added more hot water.

'You need to keep your foot in water for just a few more minutes,' Amber said after she had examined the girl. 'You have already been soaking it for about forty minutes, haven't you?'

Lara nodded. 'I've got a terrible headache. I feel awful.'

'I know you do. These things are not very pleasant, are they? The hot water should deactivate the venom and it also helps to ease the pain, but I'll give you something to take for that anyway. I think the best course of action would be for me to infiltrate an anaesthetic into the wound, and that should help tremendously. I'm going to give you an antibiotic, as well to counteract any bacteria that might be lurking there.'

She left Lara soaking her foot while she

prepared the anaesthetic, and once that was done, the nurse gently dried the area.

'All we need to do now is to put a dressing on it,' Amber said when she had finished. 'You should be feeling much better very soon.'

'It feels good already,' Lara said. 'It's such a relief. It was a horrible pain.'

'Well, next time you go wading in waters where there are stingrays, perhaps it would be a good idea to wear some kind of waterproof sandal, or at least shuffle your feet so that you can see if there are any rays lurking close by.'

She left the girl with her mother a few minutes later, and went to report back to Kyle. 'I think we have a satisfied customer back there,' she said. 'I hope all my problems are going to be as easy to solve as that one.'

Kyle laughed. 'You should be so lucky. In fact, we've just had a call to say that there's been a boating accident off the coast. We wouldn't normally expect you to go out with the crew on your first day, but the doctor who's actually on call isn't feeling so good, and the boss thought we should give you the option. How are you with lifeboats? Do you feel up to going on board to help out?'

She nodded. 'That's fine by me, if you're sure you have enough people on hand here.'

'We'll manage. Go and get kitted up in the locker room. The nurse will show you your uniform. You need to be ready to go in five minutes. The boss will meet you at the ambulance bay.'

Amber hurried to get ready, and she was waiting at the ambulance bay with a minute to spare. She looked around for the emergency vehicle, but as it came into view, her heart sank. Ethan was holding open the passenger door for her, leaning across from the driver's seat.

'Over here,' he said.

Her jaw dropped. 'Are you the boss? Don't tell me you're in charge of callouts?'

'Okay, then, I won't.' He shrugged. 'Are you going to get into the car? We don't have time to debate the issue.'

'You didn't tell me that I would be working

alongside you,' she said with a frown as she slid into the seat beside him. 'You might have warned me. I thought you worked in a different hospital. According to Martyn, you were based nearer to Honolulu.'

He started the engine and headed for the main road. 'That's true, or at least it was true, but when Martyn was taken ill I had to work closer to home so that I could take over the running of the plantation. I transferred to the local hospital.'

'You must have known we'd end up working together.'

'Not necessarily. I didn't know you were going to volunteer for the on-call work, did I? That wasn't part of the plan originally. It was just something you and Kyle worked out between you.' He checked the road conditions in the mirror and then indicated that he was turning onto the coast road. 'Anyway, what's happened has happened, and we have no real choice but to make the best of it.'

She pressed her lips together. He was right, and, no matter what her feelings were on the matter, it was time to start thinking about the work ahead. 'So tell me about this accident at sea. What can we expect?'

'Apparently, a mast snapped on a sailboat and people were injured when it fell. A woman phoned the accident in.' He sucked in a sharp breath. 'She said her husband and brother were injured, along with her young son. It looks as though her husband has come off worst because he has collapsed. The brother has some sort of head or facial injury, and the boy has a possible fractured wrist.'

'So our role is to treat them as best we can and then send them on to hospital,' she said. 'Presumably they'll be transported by lifeboat?'

He nodded. 'Yes, unless we need to transfer anyone urgently, in which case we'll call for air support. I doubt that will be necessary. They're not far off the coast, so it shouldn't take us long to get there.'

He kept his attention on the road the whole time they were speaking, and Amber could see from the rigid line of his jaw that he was unusually tense. Perhaps he was worried about what lay ahead of them and was desperate to reach the injured people as soon as was possible.

In fact, they were on board the sailboat within fifteen minutes. The lifeboat stayed alongside while Amber and Ethan tended to the injured people.

Ethan turned his attention to the man who was most seriously hurt. 'It looks as though he has abdominal injuries,' he said. His expression was grim. 'I'll put in an airway to support his breathing, but we need to stabilise his spine in case there are other injuries.'

'I'll help you with that as soon as I've seen to the other two,' Amber said. She had already decided that the man with the facial injury needed urgent attention, but the boy, Shaun, who was about twelve years old, was in a distressed state.

'Try to keep him calm,' she told his mother. 'Support his arm and wrist with a pad of rolled up clothing. I'll come and see to him as soon as possible.'

Her priority with the injured man was to put a

tube down his throat to secure his airway before swelling would prevent her from doing it. He was slipping in and out of consciousness, and on examination it appeared that his jaw was broken and that meant it was going to be a tricky process.

'What will you do?' the man's sister asked. 'I tried to stop the bleeding but I couldn't. And I was so worried—I didn't know what to do for my husband. I know the mast hit him across his abdomen but I didn't know what to do to help him.'

'Dr Brookes will look after your husband,' Amber answered. 'He's doing everything that needs to be done. As to your brother, I'm going to clear his mouth and throat of any obstruction,' she told her. 'I'll use suction to do that. I'll have to keep doing it every now and again to make sure that his throat is clear, and once I'm satisfied that his breathing is stable, I'll put a bandage around the crown of his head and his jaw to keep things in the right position.'

She was already working on him as she was speaking. She added a second bandage around his forehead to keep everything in place. 'We'll arrange for a specialist to operate on him as soon as we get back to the hospital,' she said.

As soon as she had done what was necessary, she turned her attention to the boy. 'Can you tell me what happened?' she asked him.

'I fell,' he said. He was much calmer now, and she guessed that the shock of the accident had caused his initial distress as had the pain and discomfort he'd suffered. 'Well, my dad pushed me out of the way so that I wouldn't get hurt when the mast fell. I put out my hand to stop myself falling and I felt the bones go.' He looked at his wrist and hand. 'It's an odd shape, isn't it?'

'Yes, it is. That's because the bones have cracked and moved out of place,' she explained. 'I'm going to give you something to take away the pain, and we'll put a splint on your arm so that it doesn't move and cause any more damage. When we get to the hospital, a doctor will give you an anaesthetic—something to make sure that it doesn't hurt—and then he'll put the bones back into the right position. You'll have to wear a cast for a few weeks while the bones mend.'

He nodded as though he understood, and Amber worked quickly to relieve his pain and support the wrist.

'Is my dad going to be all right?' he asked. He sent his father a surreptitious, worried look. 'And what about my uncle Sam? His face is a mess.'

'Your uncle will be much better once he's had an operation to fix the bones of his jaw in place,' she said, 'and Dr Brookes is doing everything that he can for your father.' She glanced at Ethan to see how he was coping and then looked back at the boy. 'If you're all right for the moment, Shaun, I'll go and help him.'

'Yes. Help him, please.'

Ethan was listening to his patient's heartbeat through his stethoscope at that moment. 'How is he doing?' Amber asked in an undertone.

'Not too well, by the look of things.' Ethan's mouth made a flat line. 'His heartbeat is very slow, and I suspect that there's internal bleeding. We need to get him to hospital and into surgery as soon as possible. I'm giving him intravenous fluids to ensure that he doesn't go into shock, but we have to be very careful not to overdo it and cause even more problems.'

'Shall I ring ahead and tell the trauma teams what's happening?'

'Yes. And arrange for an ambulance to meet us by the shore.' He twisted around to look at the man's son. 'I know this is hard for you,' he said. 'Your father's a good man, and his first thought was to protect you. You can be proud of him.' He studied the boy, and Amber guessed he was wondering how much information he could take on board.

'He needs an operation to repair any damage that might have been caused inside him when the mast hit him,' he said. 'We're doing everything we can to make sure that he'll come out of this all right.'

Shaun seemed to cope with that well enough. His mother put an arm around him, and they clung to each other for comfort.

Ethan turned back to his patient, and Amber could see that he was deeply concerned for him. He pressed his lips together and simply watched him for a moment, and she realised that he felt a deep empathy for the little family.

It was only then that she remembered what Martyn had told her about Ethan's parents. They had been killed in a boating accident, he'd said, when Ethan had been in his teens. Was Ethan thinking about that right now? Perhaps that accounted for the sadness in his eyes.

She knelt down beside him and laid a hand lightly on his shoulder. 'Are you all right?'

He sent her a brief sideways look. Her gaze meshed with his, and in that moment a fleeting, unspoken understanding passed between them.

'I'm fine.' With a faint inclination of his head, he indicated the man with the broken jaw. 'I see you managed to stop the bleeding. That was good work. He looked a mess, but you managed to sort things out and soothe the boy at the same time.'

'It wasn't too difficult.' She was already dialling the number for the hospital. 'We should tell the lifeboat people that we're ready to move Shaun and his mother. That will give us more room to manoeuvre. Perhaps a couple of the crew could help us move the father onto a spinal board.'

He nodded, and she set things in motion while he tended to his patient. Soon the men from the lifeboat were escorting the woman and her son from the sailboat.

'You're good at this, aren't you?' Ethan said glancing up at her. 'Calm, efficient, focussed. Perhaps my uncle was right when he thought you would slot into this job as though you were made for it. He's a people-watcher, you know. He doesn't say a lot, but it's all going on inside his head.'

All the while he was talking, he was checking his patient's vital signs, and Amber's respect for him was growing by the minute. This was a side of the man she hadn't seen before. This was the professional, the man who was dedicated to his career. She could see it in his every action. He was thorough, taking time to do a good job, making sure that his patient was stabilised before he was moved.

'Perhaps I should return the compliment,' she said. 'You've been totally focussed on what we're doing right from the start. You didn't waste a second in getting here, and you had all the equipment that you needed right on hand.'

'It's essential that you do that,' he murmured. 'The emergency car is always stocked for every journey, and we each have a pack of essential equipment. That's why yours was waiting for you when you decided to come with me. And you made up your mind fast—that was very surprising.' His gaze narrowed on her. 'But you didn't know I would be the one going along with you, did you, back then?'

She didn't answer him. Why would she rise to his bait?

The lifeboat crew came to help lift the injured man on to the stretcher, and they quickly transported both men to their vessel. From then on it was a matter of minutes before the accident victims were on their way to hospital.

Ethan followed the ambulance. He drove carefully, but fast, and she guessed he was anxious to make sure his patient was safe. They didn't speak about things that had gone wrong between them or how they were going to proceed from now on.

Amber had made her decision to work with the emergency service, and if that meant working alongside Ethan, so be it. She was through with trying to defend herself. Let him do his worst. She had the measure of her opponent, and from now on they would meet on equal terms.

Amber's working day finished just after lunch-time. It was a good arrangement, as far as she was concerned, because it gave her most of the after-noon to keep tabs on Martyn's progress, and there was still the glorious opportunity to explore the rest of this beautiful island. The one flaw was that her patients were still in surgery when she had to leave.

'I'll give you a call and let you know how they're doing,' Kyle told her. 'Ethan asked to be informed, as well. He had to go off on another emergency.'

'Thanks, Kyle. I appreciate that.' The man with abdominal injuries was her main concern, but they had been able to get to him within minutes of the accident happening, and those minutes were precious when lives were at stake.

* * *

Martyn met her at the door of the main house when she arrived there about an hour later, after taking time to freshen up back at her bungalow. He seemed to be in a thoughtful mood, as though he was preoccupied with something.

'How was your day?' he asked. 'I heard you met up with Ethan.'

'How did you know that?' She was astonished. 'I didn't know myself that we would be working together until shortly after I started my shift.'

They walked into the sitting-room. 'It was on the local news. The press were in touch with the lifeboat crew, and they broadcast it on the local radio station and on the TV.'

'Good heavens. It's a small world, isn't it?'

'It certainly is.' He sat down on an elegant cream-coloured sofa and waved a hand towards the chair opposite. 'Sit down, and tell me about your day. How did you and he get on?'

'We were fine,' she murmured. 'It came as quite a shock to me, I can tell you, to find that we were working together, but when you have to look after people who are ill or hurting, the job is really all that you have in mind. It's a bit like being on autopilot, I think.'

He looked faintly relieved. 'He's a good doctor, Ethan. His colleagues were upset when he had to leave his job at the other hospital, but they're hoping it won't be too long before he decides to go back.'

Amber sent him a guarded look. So he had known all along that Ethan had changed hospitals. Still, why would he think it mattered one way or the other to her? She had been out of work, and a job in Hawaii was a prize by any standards.

'You look as though you're mulling something over,' she said, studying him. 'I could see from your expression when you opened the door that you were preoccupied. What's troubling you? Anything in particular?'

His expression sobered. 'I'm not quite sure how to tell you this,' he said. 'It's good news for me, but I'm not sure that you will feel the same way.'

She frowned. 'Have you found someone to replace me? Is that what you're trying to say?' Perhaps he had taken on board Ethan's doubts about her and decided that since they weren't getting along, things would have to change. They hadn't drawn up a contract of any sort after all, and the only concrete things she had were the job at the hospital and her airfare home.

His brows shot up. 'Good heavens, girl. Why on earth would you think that way? Is it something Ethan said? You shouldn't take any notice of him. He has his own ideas about how things should be, but they don't always match up with mine.'

Amber stared at him. So Molly was right. He did know what was going on between her and Ethan, but he wasn't putting any store by it.

'No, it's nothing to do with Ethan.' It was only half a lie, but she censored it with herself because she didn't want anything to disrupt the harmony that existed between the two men. 'I was never quite sure why you asked me to come out here. You don't really need me. You have all these people to help you out, and you have your own doctor on the island, as well as Ethan to watch over you. I accepted because I'd really taken to you as a person, and because Hawaii seemed like the answer to my prayers.'

He gave her a thoughtful look. 'And you had split up with your boyfriend, James. I admit to feeling a bit guilty about that, because it was my own daughter who came between you…but, to be honest, I never thought you and he were right for each other.'

Her eyes widened. 'You don't miss anything, do you?'

'Well, it was fairly obvious. And that friend of yours, Sarah, told me a bit about what was going on…only because I prised it out of her, you understand. I'm a nosy soul. Always have been. Grace used to say to me, "Stop interfering. Let people get on with their own lives. They won't thank you for intruding." But I've always been the same. I need to know what's going on around me, and if I can help people out, or change things for the better, that's what I'll do. Ethan's the same in some ways. He knows what he wants and he sets out to get it.'

'Hmm.' He was certainly right about that.

Ethan had tried several devious ways to detach her from his uncle, and when they hadn't worked, he had taken a step back. She didn't imagine for a minute, though, that he had given up. 'But you still haven't told me your news. What is it?'

He frowned. 'I don't want you to be upset by this. I never thought that James was the right man for you. It seemed to me that he couldn't quite cope with your ways of handling things. You were always in control of a situation, and you were good at exams, good at your job, whereas he always seemed to be a little bit in your shadow. I'm sorry to say that, Amber, because he's a good man, just not the man for you.'

She looked at him, a slow chill creeping down her spine. 'Are you saying your news is about James? Is that what this is about?'

'I am. I'm sorry.' He leaned forward in his seat as though he wanted to be closer to her, to comfort her. 'You see, Caitlin called this morning. She said that James has asked her to marry him, and she said yes to him. They want to hold the ceremony out here on Oahu.' He frowned. 'I know how difficult that will be for you.'

Amber pulled in a sharp breath. This couldn't be happening. Not here, not now. She had come all this way to where she'd thought she was safe. And now her world was crashing down around her. How could James do this to her? It was like rubbing salt in the wound.

'When is this supposed to happen?' she asked.

'Next month. They don't want to wait. They made up their minds that this is what they want to do, and they say can fit in the wedding and honeymoon before they both start work at the university over here. Apparently James has secured a research post alongside Caitlin.'

'Oh…oh.' It was more of a shudder than a word. She felt her heart plummet to the pit of her stomach. Not only were they getting married out here, they would be living and working here, too.

Her head was in a whirl. 'I need to think about this,' she said. 'I don't know what to do. Perhaps I should go away.' She twisted around as though she would make her escape right there and then. 'I can't stay here and watch this happen.'

He began to shake his head. 'That's not the real you talking, the girl who takes control of her life and gets things sorted.'

'Oh, but it is,' she said. 'Don't you see? I'm a coward. I don't have any backbone. I ran away once, and I can do it again.'

'But you won't.' He spoke softly, his voice gentle with understanding. 'And it wasn't as though you were actually running away from James, was it? It might have seemed that way, but there were other things going on at the time.'

She stared at him dazedly. 'I don't know what you mean.'

'I don't think James was the crux of things. After all, you stood by and watched what was happening and said nothing. You could have kicked up a fuss and tried to work things out between you, but you didn't. You accepted what was going on.'

He paused. 'Why should you blame yourself for finding an easy way out? Your career had been messed up through no fault of your own. Who wouldn't have taken the opportunity to come and live in a land of sunshine and be pampered for a while? You're simply human, and you accepted the perfect solution when it was offered to you.'

She hadn't spoken and he looked at her to see if she was listening to what he said. 'Amber, please don't act hastily. It may seem like the end of the world to you right now, but it may not be as bad as you think.' He hesitated, letting his words sink in. 'Besides, I really do need you here with me, you know. A wedding is a big thing to organise, and just the thought of it makes me feel drained of energy. You have a way of revitalising me, and I don't like to ask this of you, but this is my daughter, and I have to give her my support. I can't do it on my own, Amber. Please don't run away again.'

'Run away?' Ethan's voice ricocheted around the room as he pushed open the door. 'Why would she be running anywhere?' He walked towards them, looking from one to the other, a deep frown drawing his brows together. 'What's going on?'

Amber stood up, a wave of nausea threatening to overwhelm her. She wasn't at all sure what to make of Martyn's announcement, but to have Ethan witness her discomfiture was more than she could bear right now.

'This has nothing whatever to do with you,' she said. 'This is a private conversation between me and your uncle.' She knew it was the wrong thing to say as soon as she'd said it, it was ill mannered and intolerable, but her mind was reeling in shock, and Ethan's arrival had sent her spinning into a vortex of confusion.

Why did he have to turn up like a bad penny when she was at her lowest ebb? How could she fight her demons with him around? Wasn't he the worst demon of all?

She needed to get away from here and go somewhere to lick her wounds in private. Why should Ethan witness her downward spiral? It wasn't fair. Life wasn't fair. It was full of trip wires and traps that had been laid for the unwary and she was finding herself tangled up in every one of them.

'Amber? What's happened? What's wrong?'

Ethan was frowning, his gaze homing in on her as though he would pin her down right there and make her give him an answer.

Amber stared at him, caught in the glitter of those blue eyes like a trapped animal. He, of all people, would rejoice in her downfall.

Then she looked at Martyn, and saw how pale he had become, and her heart crumpled. He was ill, and it was up to her to ensure his well-being, but she had let him down at the first hurdle. His glow of happiness had been blotted out by a grey cloud, and it was all her fault.

'Martyn, I'm sorry,' she said. 'I didn't mean to cast a shadow on your good news. I just need to think this through.'

'It's all right,' he murmured. 'I understand.'

'I'm glad someone does,' Ethan said in a brisk tone, 'because I certainly don't. Is anyone going to enlighten me?' He glared at both of them, his brows drawing together in a dark line, his stare threatening retribution.

'Not now, Ethan,' Martyn said wearily. 'Just give it a while, will you?'

Amber had been glued to the spot, but she suddenly found that strength had surged back into her legs. She turned away and hurried out of the room.

CHAPTER EIGHT

'YOU still haven't told me what caused the upset the other day.' Ethan threw Amber a sideways glance. He was at the wheel of the emergency vehicle, heading at top speed towards the coast, and all Amber could see of the landscape was a blur of trees and blue sky. 'Why would you be thinking of running away?'

'Would you just concentrate on your driving instead of asking questions?' She gritted her teeth. 'I'd as soon get there in one piece.'

'There's nothing wrong with my driving.' He raised a dark brow. 'I took an advanced driving test and passed with flying colours.'

'Yes, and I suspect *flying* might be the operative word.'

His mouth quirked in response, but Amber was relieved when he slowed down to a pace that she could cope with. 'Is that better?' he asked.

'Much better. Thank you.' She began to breathe more easily. 'I know we have to get there quickly, but there's a limit to how much risk I want to take.' She frowned. 'The lifeguards are already on the scene, aren't they, and they're trained in resuscitation methods?'

'That's true, but we're closer at hand than anyone else, and if we can get there before the ambulance, the boy has a greater chance of survival.' He glanced at her. 'I didn't mean to scare you. Are you okay?'

'I'm fine.'

By now he was slowing down even more, turning the car on to the slipway used for towing boats on and off the beach. He applied the brakes.

Amber had the passenger door open as soon as the vehicle stopped, and then she sprinted across the flat, smooth sand to where she could see the lifeguards at work. Ethan kept pace with her.

'How's he doing?' Amber asked the lifeguard

who was working on the boy. She put her medical bag down on the sand.

'Not too well. We brought him out of the water as quickly as we could, but he was already unconscious. We've been working on him for a couple of minutes and there's been no change.'

The lifeguard continued with chest compressions while Ethan went down on his knees and started to assess the boy's condition.

Amber guessed the child was about ten years old, and there was a graze across his temple where the surfboard had hit him as he overturned in the water. His worried parents were standing nearby, looking ashen faced and weepy.

She checked for a pulse. 'It's barely discernible.'

Ethan quickly introduced an endotracheal tube into the boy's throat. 'I need suction,' he said, but Amber was already by his side, ready to clear the boy's airway and enable Ethan to attach the oxygen supply.

Once the child's airway was assured, Ethan inserted a gastric tube so that they could draw water or debris from his stomach. Amber started to set up two intravenous lines, so that he could be given fluids and medication, while Ethan taped electrodes in place on the boy's chest so that his heart rhythm could be monitored.

'Let's get him warmed up,' Ethan said, as soon as they were finished. They could already hear the sound of the ambulance siren in the distance, and by the time the paramedics arrived their patient was wrapped in a blanket. They worked together to carefully transfer him to a body board to protect his spine. Then they strapped him securely in place.

Ethan handed over their patient into the care of the paramedics, while Amber tried to comfort the boy's tearful parents. 'We'll get him to hospital straight away, and the medical team will take over as soon as he arrives. They'll take good care of him.' She knew that the boy's problems were far from over. He would need careful nursing to ensure that his heart rate and blood pressure returned to normal, and any lung complications could be averted or dealt with.

'I'd like to follow up on him at the hospital,'

she told Ethan, when the ambulance started to pull away. 'We don't have any immediate calls to make, do we?'

'No. I'm with you on that one,' he murmured. 'I always follow up on the patients I've brought in. I like to know what happens to them.'

They went back to the car and Ethan set the engine in motion. 'It's uplifting whenever there's a good outcome.'

'Like the man who collapsed on his boat after he was hit by the mast.' Amber smiled. 'I heard he'll be coming out of hospital soon. And his brother-in-law is on the mend, too.'

'It turned out well in the end, didn't it? I felt sorry for the young lad. It was a scary situation for him, and he was clearly worried about his father, but he managed to hold it together very well.'

Amber glanced at him, wondering whether she should ask him about what had happened to his own parents or whether it would be best to leave it alone.

In the end she said softly, 'I guessed you were worried for the family and that you understood exactly what they were going through. Martyn told me what happened to your parents. It must have brought it all home to you.'

He nodded and didn't seem to mind that she had brought up the subject. 'I was a little older than the boy when the accident happened, so perhaps I was better able to cope with it. Like him, I was on board the boat at the time, and it was a frightening experience. We were caught up in a sudden storm at sea, and the waves were higher than any I'd ever seen. I think the boat must have been blown off course, and there was a problem with the onboard electronics. My father managed to radio for help, but he was tossed against the framework of the cabin and suffered a head injury. My mother and I went to help him, but she collapsed. They said later that she must have suffered a heart attack.'

Amber closed her eyes briefly. 'I'm so sorry,' she said. 'That must have been dreadful for you.'

He grimaced. 'I suppose I was luckier than most. My uncle took me in and looked after me as if I was his own. He said I was like the son he never had… And Grace, my aunt, was like a mother to me. I could never get over the loss of my parents, but Martyn and Grace made my life whole again.'

'It must make you very sad to see him so ill.' She frowned. 'I felt bad that I upset him the other day. It grieves me to think that I might have been the cause of him having a relapse.'

'You didn't do anything to make his condition worse,' Ethan murmured. He turned the car on to the road leading to the hospital. 'His heart is weak, and it's only the tablets he's taking that are helping him to keep it all together. I knew some time ago that things were bad, and I didn't want him to go over to the U.K. because I thought it was too risky. I warned him, but he wanted to see how Caitlin was doing, and he was determined to look in on the U.K. offices to make sure things were shipshape.'

'Even so, it can't have helped when I reacted the way I did.'

He drove into the hospital car park and threw her a sideways glance. 'What was it all about? I know he told you that Caitlin was getting married, but why would that cause you any problems?'

He parked the car and cut the engine. Then he remained still, waiting for her answer.

She sighed. 'She's marrying my ex-boyfriend…only he wasn't an ex until he met her.'

He frowned. 'So you and James were an item? How long had you been together?'

'About a year.'

His eyes widened. 'So it wasn't a passing fancy. No wonder you were upset at the news. That must have caused you a few qualms. And did Martyn know this the whole time?'

'Yes, apparently he did.'

'No wonder you took Martyn up on his offer to come over here. It must have seemed like a heaven-sent opportunity.' He gave a soft whistle, thinking things through, and she sent him a sharp look.

'Don't gloat,' she said. 'I didn't come here with any designs on your uncle, neither did I develop any ulterior motive. I was out of work through no fault of my own, and I was ensured a job out here. You've had me wrong the whole time.'

'Have I?' He gave her a thoughtful, brooding look. 'It still doesn't account for my uncle inviting you over here and setting you up in a place of your own. He'd have treated you like a regular princess if he'd had his own way.'

'Which he didn't—and, like I said, don't gloat.'

He held up his hands as though to admit defeat. 'I'm not rejoicing in your misfortune. I wouldn't do something like that.' He studied her for a moment or two. 'So how do you feel about James coming over here now that you've had time to get used to the idea?'

'Humiliated, embarrassed, hurt—how would you expect me to feel? He threw me over for another woman, and I don't know how I'm supposed to deal with that. Maybe you have some ideas about what I should do. You seem to have plenty of ideas about everything else.'

He blinked, jerking back a little in his seat. 'Whoa. Don't pin this one on me. I'm just trying to work out exactly what's going on here.'

'Well, I'm not going to run away, that's for sure. I know you'd probably be glad if I chose to do that, but I realised that it was out of the question as soon as I saw Martyn relapse. He's getting weaker by the day, and I don't want to be the cause of any further downward spiral. I'm sorry if my staying here doesn't suit you.'

'I didn't say I thought you should leave.' He gave her a direct look, a glimmer of light starting up in the depths of his eyes. 'If I remember correctly, what I actually said was I thought you should turn your attention towards me. That way we both stand a chance of getting what we want.'

She glowered at him. 'You're impossible,' she said, reaching for the handle and pushing the door open. 'I can't talk to you when you're like this.'

She slid out of her seat and started to walk towards the doors of the accident and emergency department. She would concentrate her attention on the boy who had nearly drowned. He, at least, was worthy of her anxiety.

The boy gradually recovered over the next few hours, and the following day the doctors were able to remove the tube from his throat. He sat up and began to pay attention to his surroundings, and his parents were exhilarated to have their son back.

Over the next few weeks, Amber concentrated on trying to boost Martyn's strength. She made slight changes to his medication, giving him diuretics to lower the pressure in his arteries and heart, along with tablets to improve the heart's pumping ability. Gradually, he seemed to be better able to cope.

The wedding plans went ahead, and Amber did her best to ignore the preparations going on around her. The wedding was to be held on Martyn's land, with a terraced and grassed area close to the beach set aside for the actual ceremony. A wedding planner came to organise the seating arrangements, and soon there were visits from flower arrangers, caterers and all the other people who would be involved in making this a wedding to remember.

James and Caitlin arrived home the day before the ceremony was due to take place. Martyn embraced both of them and invited them into the house where Molly was busy laying out a welcome home feast in the dining-room.

Ethan greeted Caitlin like a long-lost sister, giving her a hug and at the same time lifting her off the ground and twirling her around in and exuberant show of affection. 'It's good to see you again,' he said. 'Congratulations on the new job. When do you start?'

She answered him, talking excitedly about all the changes that were taking place in her life. 'It was such good fortune that James managed to get a job in clinical research alongside me. It was what we both wanted.'

Ethan acknowledged that, and turned to James. 'So, James,' he said, giving him the once-over, 'you're going to tie the knot and whisk my cousin away to the Caribbean for your honeymoon, are you? You must be a pretty fast worker. You only met a short time ago, didn't you?'

James nodded. Perhaps he became aware of Amber standing a short distance away because he sent her a cautious glance, before answering Ethan in a low tone. 'It was more of a love-at-first-sight kind of thing,' he said, shifting his gaze to Caitlin by his side.

Caitlin slid her hand into his. 'We both knew right away that we were made for each other.' She, too, glanced towards Amber, a worried look on her face.

'I guessed it must be something like that,' Ethan said. 'And, of course, being able to connect with both of you through the video link at the hospital it meant that I already had the chance to get to know James.' He moved towards Amber, who had been helping Molly set platters of food on the table. 'It's how I first came across Amber, too.'

Amber gave a faint smile, acknowledging that. He was making an effort to include her in the conversation, and that was probably more for Martyn's sake than anything else, since his uncle was looking a bit fraught about the situation when he thought no one was looking at him.

But Ethan took her completely by surprise with his next move. He slid an arm around her shoulders and drew her close to him. 'She's the light of my life.'

The pressure of his arm about her slowly increased, as though he was giving her a hidden warning not to try to pull away. And then he looked down into her eyes with the expression of a man who was totally in love. Only Amber wasn't fooled for a moment. She could read the hidden message in those glittering eyes, and it was telling her that she should go along with this pretence, not only for her sake but for Martyn's, as well.

She gazed up at him. He was way out of order, wrapping her close this way and crushing the softness of her curves against his long body. If she could have aimed a surreptitious kick at his ankle without giving rise to suspicion, she would have, but everyone was watching them intently, and she had no choice but to smile through this mockery of a love match.

It was bad enough that he was teasing her this way, but even worse was her unwilling response. Ethan's hand seared her skin where it rested on the curve of her shoulder. He let it glide downwards until it rested lightly on the curve of her hip, and she felt the instant clamour of her nerve endings as sensation rocketed through her. He knew exactly what he was doing. With one gentle caress he fired up her senses as though she was the candle to his flame, and her whole body went into meltdown. How could he torment her this way? Why wouldn't he leave her be?

But she knew the answer to that, didn't she? He was putting his uncle's mind at rest and wiping away any guilt that might linger in his cousin's mind at the same time.

She could see that Martyn was pleased that they were supposedly over their differences and heading for something more meaningful. There was a glimmer of amusement in his eyes. If only he knew the truth of the matter...

Still, perhaps it was better this way. He could see his daughter married with a clear conscience, and his blessing would go with them when they set off for the Caribbean.

She carefully detached herself from Ethan's embrace. 'I promised Molly I'd help with the food,' she said. 'Excuse me, will you?

Caitlin followed her a short time later, coming

into the kitchen and looking anxiously across the table towards her. 'I'm so glad you've managed to find happiness for yourself,' she said. 'You must think I'm a terrible person.' There was a catch in her voice as she added, 'I didn't know, to begin with that you and James were a couple. If I had done, I probably wouldn't have let things go as far as they did. By the time I found out, it was too late. I'd fallen for him completely.' She looked at Amber, her gaze sincere, apologetic. 'Can you forgive me?'

'I never blamed you,' Amber said. 'You were going through a very difficult time, with your father being seriously ill, and I could see that you turned to James for comfort. It doesn't matter. Don't worry about it.' She was thoughtful for a moment or two. 'Perhaps he and I were never really suited anyway. We got on very well together, like true friends, but there has to be more if you want to sustain a relationship.'

Caitlin seemed to take comfort in that. 'I'm glad you don't feel too badly towards us,' she said. They spoke for a while longer about various things and then she glanced around the kitchen. 'Molly has done us proud again, hasn't she? Shall I take that bowl of rice through to the dining room?'

'Yes, she has. Thanks, that would be helpful.'

Caitlin went back into the dining room and Amber gathered up a tray of nibbles and headed after her. She saw James and Ethan talking to one another as though they were old friends, and she decided that she would like nothing more than to slip away at the first opportunity.

She couldn't, though. They were ready to sit down and eat together, and the talk was all about the wedding the next day.

'You brought your dress in London, I heard,' Molly said, looking at Caitlin and placing a basket of crusty rolls on the table. 'I can't wait to see it.'

Ethan came and sat next to Amber. He offered her a dish of chilled tropical fruits. 'This is your favourite starter, isn't it? Well, next to Molly's scrumptious prawn cocktail, at least. What's your fancy today?'

She looked at him from under her lashes. How did he know about her favourite food? Was he a people watcher, like his uncle? Or was it simply a case of getting to know the enemy? 'You don't need to keep up a pretence with me,' she said, keeping her voice low. 'I believe James already has the message. That stunt you pulled earlier was enough to grab his attention—and everyone else's too. Even Martyn fell for it.'

'You can't have too much of a good thing,' Ethan murmured. 'Let's make sure they swallow it hook, line and sinker, shall we? Then the wedding will go off smoothly and the young couple will go off happily on their honeymoon.'

'I'm not playing your games,' she muttered under her breath. 'Enough is enough.'

'Enough?' He lifted a dark brow. 'Believe me, angel, I haven't even started yet.'

She looked up at him then, and he smiled at her, his mouth curving in a way that found its mark, a bone-melting, heat-seeking-missile kind of smile that laid waste to her defences and left her floundering.

He was incorrigible. Worst of all, she had the feeling he would be true to his word, and her knees grew weak at the thought. How could she withstand the onslaught of his carefully prepared manoeuvres? Heat pooled in her abdomen at his mere smile, so how on earth could she cope with a full-blooded ambush?

On the morning of the wedding, the bustle of preparations moved up several notches. The caterers set out a banquet fit for a king. There were Caesar and Waldorf salads and fruit starters, a selection of appetisers, which included spinach and cheese brochettes, and there was filet mignon, along with spiced chicken and seafood dishes. For dessert there were all kinds of delicious sweets to choose from…tropical fruits, whipped cream and chocolate mousse were just a few.

Outside, in the grounds of the house, rows of elegant white-painted chairs were set out on the lawns by the terrace, and standing columns adorned with splendid flower arrangements had been placed alongside the seating area. There was a bridal archway festooned with fragrant roses, and to one side was an area laid out with tables and chairs where people would sit and eat after the ceremony.

Beyond the immediate area, the curve of the bay provided a jewelled backcloth, where the glitter of sunlight on the blue ocean vied with white ribbons of surf that were left by the gentle waves rolling up on the beach. A cluster of palm trees would provide the setting for photographs of the bride and groom, and altogether Amber couldn't think of a lovelier way for a couple to be married.

'How are you doing?' Ethan asked softly, coming alongside her as she stood on a low promontory, breathing in the salt tang of the air and gazing out at the ocean. 'Just a short time now, and everyone will be taking their seats for the ceremony. How are you coping with all that?'

Her mouth made a crooked shape. 'Are you afraid that when the minister says, "Does anyone here know any good reason why this couple should not be married?" I'll interrupt and say, "Yes, it should have been me"?'

He laughed. 'I'm pretty sure you wouldn't go that far.' He slid his arms around her. 'But how do you really feel?'

'I don't know,' she answered truthfully. 'It's very strange, but I don't feel anything. Perhaps I just want it to be over, so that life can get back to normal, or at least as normal as it can be out here when my home is in the U.K. My whole world is upside down right now.'

'Well, we have a whole day of celebrations ahead of us, good food, music, dancing. Let me help you through that, at least. We can think about getting back to normal later.'

'I don't need help,' she said. 'I'm okay, and I just want to be left to deal with things my own way.'

He sucked in his breath. 'Oh, I don't think that's a good idea at all. You have way too many devils to fight…least of all the fact that your ex-boyfriend might wonder how you feel about all this.' He gazed beyond her to the house where all the preparations were going on at a fast pace. 'You haven't spoken to him about that yet, have you?'

'I haven't had the chance. Obviously, we talked

before I left England for Hawaii, but the wedding plans came as a complete shock.' She listened to the waves lapping at the shore, lulling her with their own soft, calming refrain.

'I expect he wants to know that all is forgiven…but maybe you've moved on since then?' He drew her closer to him, winding his arms around her so that there was no escape. Then he lowered his head to hers and in the next moment he had claimed her lips, crushing their softness in a kiss that was more thorough and passionate than anything she'd ever experienced.

His hands slowly stroked the length of her spine, trailing over the curve of her hips, and a wave of delicious sensation coursed through her. It felt as though her entire body was fused with his in an explosion of pleasure that left her weak with desire.

How was it that he could make her feel this way? She had never been so emotionally out of control before. It was as if he had lit a spark within her that flared briefly and within seconds had ignited a conflagration. Her whole body yearned for him. She needed him. She loved the way he was holding her, kissing her, thrilling her with his gently stroking hands. He made her feel cherished, as though they were the only two people in the world and there was no need for anything else.

And then he was slowly releasing her and she stared up at him in a haze of bewilderment. She wanted that sweet bond to go on for ever, and yet he was carefully easing himself away from her

He looked beyond her and said quietly, 'Hello, there, James. Forgive us for cluttering up your parade. You must be anxious for the ceremony to go ahead. Not long now, huh?'

'That's right.' James looked uncertain, and more than a little bemused, and Amber gazed at him in shock. She had not heard him approach.

He was halfway along the path towards them, but he had half turned as though he had started to go back the way he had come. She wondered if he would have walked away without disturbing them if Ethan had not spoken. Perhaps he thought neither of them had seen him, being engrossed in that kiss.

'I just came to see if Amber was all right,' James added, turning to face them full on. 'So much was going on yesterday and this morning, and we haven't been able to talk up to now. I didn't want to go through the ceremony without at least saying a few words, but it looks as though I needn't have worried.'

She found her voice. 'I'm fine, James,' she said huskily. 'I wish you and Caitlin all the luck in the world. I'm sure you'll have a wonderful marriage.'

'Thank you.'

By her side, Ethan maintained a watchful, cautious look over James. His hand still lay possessively on the curve of her hip, and all at once it dawned on Amber that Ethan's actions were not as innocent as he would have her believe.

He must have known all along that James was heading towards them. Perhaps he had seen him come out of the house.

His actions had to have been deliberate from the first. He had meant James to see them kiss. This whole episode had been for James's benefit.

The knowledge washed over her like a cold

shower of rain. She felt cheated, filled with dismay because her foolish mind had let her believe for just a small space of time that Ethan might actually care for her.

Instead, though, it was all a game to him. A ruse to ensure that his cousin would go off contentedly into her marriage and James would harbour no doubts that Amber's feelings for him had been well and truly extinguished.

That last was the only part that gave her solace. She watched James walk away from them towards the house, and it came on her with stunning clarity that her relationship with him had never been the real thing. It had been a friendship built on tender affection and mutual respect, but it would never have lasted a lifetime.

It seemed that Ethan was the only man who could make her feel truly alive and at the same time full of emotional contradictions. He confused her, provoked her, startled in her feelings she'd never known she possessed, and through it all he sparked a fire that raged throughout her body, an all-consuming inferno that threatened to destroy her.

For the unpalatable truth was that Ethan didn't love her. He was simply playing a part, and when the game was over, she would be the loser.

'I'm going back to the house,' she told him now. 'Molly asked me to help her give out the corsages, and I still have to change and get ready for the ceremony.'

Over the next hour, guests began to arrive, along with the minister who was to conduct the marriage ceremony, and before too long the formal proceedings began.

Caitlin wore an exquisite dress of white silk, and James was splendid in a crisp, perfectly tailored suit. They made their marriage vows while Amber looked on and realised that she was actually pleased for them.

She had expected that she might feel empty inside or lost in some way as she saw James married, but instead she was completely at ease. Her thoughts had an unsettling way of dwelling on a different man entirely, a man with jet-black hair and startlingly blue eyes, but perhaps that was because Ethan was by her side, and she was conscious the whole time of him surreptitiously watching her.

With the ceremony over, the celebrations began. They ate at the tables on the terrace and listened to the traditional speeches, and after a while musicians moved into place on the specially erected dais and began to play lilting Hawaiian music.

Amber danced alongside the women in the wedding party, and there was a good deal of fun and laughter as they practised the traditional hula. Molly put a circlet of flowers in Amber's hair and placed a lei around her neck.

'Now you dance, see, flowing movements of your arms and hips, and you become one with the waving palm trees and the flowing sea.'

Amber was wearing a cotton top and a softly draped skirt that flowed around her legs as she danced barefoot with the rhythm of the music.

'They say the hula was first danced by Hi'iaka, goddess of Hawaii, of the hills, the lands, the cliffs and caves,' Molly said. 'She was given the task of bringing home the love of her sister's life, Lohi'au, but of course things went wrong, and her sister, Pele, wreaked havoc. Pele was the goddess of the volcano, the spirit of molten lava, and Hi'iaka tried to appease her with the dance… So, you see, the hula is more than just a dance. It tells a story, and you become part of the story when you dance.'

Several of the male guests came to join them in the dancing, and Amber had no shortage of partners. Then Ethan came to claim her for himself, and the next few hours became a blur of sensation, of being held in his arms and swaying gently to the sensual rhythm of the music, of feeling the warmth of his body next to hers. She loved the way he nuzzled the soft skin of her throat, the way his hands lightly caressed her.

She wished the closeness were for real, that it was something more than just a pretence, because she was fast discovering that whenever she was with him she felt as though she could take on the world. All was well, and nothing could ripple the reservoir of contentment she felt in his arms.

The cherished moments came to an end, though, when James and Caitlin prepared to leave.

Perhaps that was just as well, because with each hour she spent with Ethan she found herself being sucked deeper and deeper into a whirlpool of emotion that she couldn't comprehend. How could she feel this way about a man who teased and mocked her and had voiced his suspicions about her from the first?

The bride and groom left in the middle of the evening while the celebrations were still in full swing, and the guests went to see them depart. The couple left in the bridal car for the hotel where they would spend the night before setting off for their honeymoon the following day.

Amber waved them off alongside Martyn, wishing them good fortune and showering the wedding car with flower petals.

When they had disappeared out of sight, Martyn turned back to his guests. '*Mahalo nui loa na ho'olaule'a me la kaua,*' he said. 'Thank you for celebrating with us. My daughter is starting a new life with her new husband, and I'm sure we all wish them well. Please stay and enjoy the party. The dancing and the music will go on until the early hours.'

Amber glanced at him as he stepped back from the driveway and turned to walk along the footpath. 'How are you coping? You look very happy. This must have been a wonderful day for you.'

He nodded. 'It's been a good day, but I'm tired now. I shan't stay for the rest of the party. I'm glad I was able to see her settled. I think she's made a good match.' He sent her a thoughtful look. 'And how is it with you? You seem to be bearing up—perhaps you realised that he wasn't the right man for you after all. You've much too feisty a spirit to be content with James for long.'

'I expect you're right.' She walked with him back to the house. 'I'm inclined to say what I think, and I haven't the patience to bide my time or debate the whys and wherefores of a situation if I see something that needs doing.'

Martyn smiled. 'That sounds a lot like Ethan's character…though I've noticed of late he's played his cards close to his chest. I know he made out that you and he had something going between you at lunch yesterday, but I'm guessing that was for Caitlin's benefit. His intentions were good, I'm sure. And it had the desired effect. Both Caitlin and James seemed reassured.'

She studied him for a moment or two. 'Nothing much gets by you, does it?' She smiled. She might have known he wouldn't be fooled.

'That's true. I know Ethan too well, and I've pretty much picked up on your vibes over these last few weeks. Don't think too harshly of him, will you? I have a feeling you and he are actually more in tune with one another than you think. It would make me very happy if you and he were to get together.'

Her eyes widened. 'You wouldn't be trying to play matchmaker, would you?' She wouldn't put it past him. There was a lot going on in Martyn's head, much more than he let on.

'I wouldn't dream of it,' he said, but there was a wicked glint in his eyes that told her he was fibbing. 'Anyway, I'd be wasting my time, wouldn't I? Ethan does exactly as he pleases…

and you're more than a match for him when it comes to down to it.' His mouth curved. 'Caitlin, now…she takes after her mother, gentle, uncontroversial, a peacemaker. It seems to me that she and James are very well suited.'

Amber helped him to his room. 'Would you like me to get you a hot drink to help you sleep?'

He shook his head. 'I shan't have any difficulty in sleeping, even with the party going on,' he said. He eased himself into his bedside chair. 'Ethan will wind things up when the time comes. He knows what to do and he always does the right thing. I feel secure leaving everything in his hands…the plantation, the house… He knows what needs to be done.'

Amber sent him an anxious look. His thoughts seemed to be drifting, and he wasn't making much sense. Perhaps he was more tired than he realised. 'I'll ask Ben to come and help you to bed,' she murmured. 'Is there anything I can get for you?'

'Nothing, my dear. I have everything I could want. It's been a good life.'

Amber frowned. She stayed for a while,

waiting as he drifted into sleep. Then she carefully checked his pulse and tried to reassure herself that all was well with him.

A few minutes later, she hurried downstairs and asked Ben if he would go and help him prepare for bed.

'You look worried,' Ethan said, catching up with her as she left the kitchen. 'Is everything all right with my uncle?'

She shook her head. 'I think so, but I'm not sure. He's not quite himself but, then, it has been a long day, and a momentous one, for him. I think he must be very tired.'

'I'll look in on him in a while,' Ethan murmured. 'Are you going to stay and enjoy the rest of the evening?'

'I'll stay for a while,' she said. 'I want to make sure that Martyn is all right.'

'Good. Maybe we could keep each other company. A few more dances in the moonlight would be good, don't you think? It would be a crime to let such a beautiful night go to waste.'

'That's true enough…but you really don't have

to play games with me any more, Ethan. James and Caitlin aren't here any more, and your uncle has gone to bed. You can relax and be yourself.'

'I was never playing games,' he murmured. 'Don't you know that?' His blue gaze travelled over her, sweeping down from the burnished chestnut of her hair, over her slender, feminine curves and along the length of her shapely legs. 'I was deadly serious. Always.'

Amber's eyes widened. 'Always?'

His mouth made a crooked shape. 'When it comes to knowing what I want, I wouldn't let anything get in my way…and I've wanted you from the first, Amber.'

A ripple of heat washed over her, bringing soft colour to her cheeks. She shook her head. 'But you're talking about purely physical feelings,' she said, 'and I think there has to be a lot more on offer than that.'

She wasn't going to let him bamboozle her with his smooth way of talking. He'd been messing with her emotions ever since she'd arrived in Hawaii. She had the notion he'd be more than content with a wild, passionate affair, and when those initial feelings fizzled out, it would be a simple case of 'goodbye and thanks'. The fact that her heart would be broken into little pieces wouldn't matter a jot to him, would it?

His eyes took on a glimmer of amusement. 'Does there? I'd say physical had a lot going for it.'

'Yes, and so does self-respect…my self-respect.'

He laughed softly as she brushed past him on her way to the terrace. His hand whipped out and circled her wrist like a lasso. 'You can run, but you can't hide,' he warned. 'You stir my blood with every move you make, and the temperature's rising.'

'Then I suggest you go and take a cold shower, Ethan,' she murmured. She wrenched her arm free from his grasp. 'It'll do you the world of good.'

She hurried outside, glad of the faint breeze that fanned her cheeks, but all the while she was conscious of Ethan's blue gaze searing her flesh and his gentle laughter echoed inside her head.

CHAPTER NINE

'I CAN'T imagine what Mr Martyn's up to,' Molly said. 'He's had these lawyers come up from town to see him. They've been shut in the study with him this past hour.' She placed a steaming pot of coffee on the dining table, and added a jug of cream alongside a dish of brown sugar.

'It does seem a little odd,' Ethan murmured, helping himself to savoury rice from a dish on the hotplate at the side of the dining room. 'He usually tells me what's going on, but all he's said is that he needs to make some firm arrangements concerning the plantation.'

'Surely he would tell you what those arrangements were?' Amber queried lightly. She chose a light salad for herself, and some pasta blended with tomatoes and aromatic herbs.

They went to sit at the table, while Molly disappeared into the kitchen. 'I know he's anxious that if anything should happen to him, all the legalities are firmly in place,' Ethan commented. 'He knows that I will take care of things since I own half anyway, but he wants to make sure that Caitlin's interests are assured. He'd already set up a trust fund for her, but I imagine, now that she's married, he feels he needs to tie up any loose ends.'

'That sounds logical enough to me.' Amber frowned. 'It's worrying me that he's doing all this, though. Even though his illness has slowed him down these last few months, he was always lively in his mind, but now he seems to be a little withdrawn, preoccupied almost, and very weary. I can't change his medication any more… There's nothing else I can give him that will help. Instead, I have to look on and see him growing weaker by the day.'

'You shouldn't blame yourself in any way.' Ethan sent her a quick look. 'You've done as much if not more than anyone could. I don't think he's concerned by what's happening to him. In fact, he seems more content than he's ever been.'

'Perhaps you're right.' She poured coffee for both of them and paused for a moment to savour the hot liquid. 'He was certainly happy to see Caitlin settled. He was so pleased when she sent him the photos of her Caribbean honeymoon, and he told me he really likes the way she's decorated their new house in town. It's quite close to the university where they'll both be working, he said.'

Ethan nodded. 'They're holding a house-warming party some time this week, aren't they?'

'Tomorrow evening.' She sent him a wry glance. 'Seems to me you need a secretary to remind you of all these things.'

He chuckled. 'Why would I bother when I have you and Molly to remind me what's going on? And if I wasn't there on time, Caitlin would soon be on the phone, asking me what had happened.' He shot her a look from half-closed eyes. 'Seems to me I'm surrounded by women who think it's my life's work to keep appointments.'

'You should count yourself lucky to be on the receiving end of all that attention,' she retorted. 'Though from what Martyn told me, you've never been short of women wanting to stick around.' She frowned. 'He said it was something of a problem, so it's probably no wonder you were suspicious of me when we first met.' She looked at him from under her lashes. 'Perhaps you still feel that way?'

He paused in the act of spearing prawns with his fork and studied her for a moment or two. 'Actually, it was more a case of overwhelming jealousy than suspicion. I had a pretty bad case of wanting what Martyn prized for himself.' His blue gaze meshed with hers.

She sat back in her chair, her eyes growing large. 'You had it all wrong.' She was quiet for a moment, a line knotting her brow. 'Martyn's a good-hearted man who saw a way to help me out. He acted out of benevolence, that's all.'

Ethan shrugged. 'Whatever his motives, I could see right away all the qualities that Martyn saw in you. You're kind, thoughtful, a brilliant doctor, beautiful, and decisive, too. You don't hang around waiting for things to happen, you think things through, decide on a course of action, and away you go.' His mouth curved. 'You and he are very much alike.'

'Perhaps that's why he took to me.' She stirred the pasta with her fork. 'You're a lot like him, too, only with a tougher exterior.'

He put a hand over his chest as if he was in pain. 'I'm a mere mortal. If you cut me, don't I bleed?'

'Pish.' She made a short, derisory sound. 'I doubt it. You'd never allow anyone to get that close. Your armour's intact, not a chink to be seen anywhere. How else have you managed to keep all those women at bay?'

His eyes half closed, his gaze narrowing on her. 'Maybe I never met one that I'd trust enough with the key to my heart. I can definitely be hurt too, you know.'

'Is that so?' She looked at him guardedly, not sure how she felt about another woman trampling over the man she was growing closer to day by day. 'Has someone wounded you?'

He picked up his coffee cup and held it in both hands for a while, staring at the dark liquid, but she sensed he wasn't really seeing it. 'My family was taken from me,' he said. 'First my mother, who I loved dearly, and then Grace, who cared for me as her own and teased me and made me smile again.' He pulled in a shuddery breath and then swallowed some of the coffee. 'I let two lovely, good-natured women into my heart, and they were ripped from me. I told myself I would be very careful who I ever let in from then on.'

She gave a soft sigh. 'I can't imagine what it must be like to go through that. I've always had my parents close at hand.' She ran a fingertip lightly around the rim of her cup, giving herself time to think. 'Of course, Martyn must have suffered along with you when he lost Grace. I'm assuming his parents lived long and healthy lives?' She looked at him for confirmation, and he nodded cautiously.

'They did, though his parents divorced when he was a youngster, and his mother married again, so you might say he's had a chequered life.'

'You wouldn't think so, from all that he's achieved. He said his grandfather started the plantation... How did you come to own half of it?'

He put his cup down. 'It was partly an inheritance from my parents. My father took an interest in it along with Martyn, and the rest became mine because I bought into it. I learned a lot about how to cultivate land over the years, and it was always taken for granted that I would follow the family tradition, but I wanted to go into medicine. After what happened to my mother and Grace, I wanted to learn how to take care of people. I needed to know that I could do something to make their lives better.'

She put down her fork and laid her hand gently on top of his. 'You do that every day,' she said softly. 'I've seen the way you handle the most difficult cases, and you're very skilled at what you do.'

He made a rueful face. 'But not skilled enough to help my uncle. I wish I could find a miracle of modern medicine that would make him whole again.'

They both knew that wasn't going to happen,

and by mutual consent they turned to other topics of conversation over the next few minutes.

They were finishing off dessert as Martyn came out of his study and saw the lawyers on their way out to their cars. When he came back, he looked like a cat that had licked the cream. 'That's all sorted, then,' he said, coming into the dining-room.

'What's sorted?' Ethan dipped his fork into a melt-in-the-mouth banana coconut cake, before glancing up at his uncle.

'Oh, tidying up a few odds and ends. There were some minor alterations to be made to Caitlin's trust fund, and a couple of papers I needed to sign to secure a piece of land for the plantation. I wanted to expand the coffee growing side of things, and I've been after that land for some time. Anyway, it's all done now, and I'm well pleased.' He looked from one to the other, smiling, and then glanced at the sideboard where the dishes on the hotplate were steaming gently.

'Have you two saved me some lunch? I hope you haven't polished off all the chicken... And there had better be some of that banana cake left.' He looked pointedly at Ethan's rapidly vanishing dessert.

Ethan immediately looked guilty. 'Ah… banana cake… Now, that could be a problem. You do know it's my favourite, don't you? I actually crave it sometimes.'

Martyn frowned and ran his glance over the table. Coming towards them, he lifted up a ceramic cover and peered at the cake stand underneath. 'Hah,' he said, giving Ethan a narrowed look before his mouth curved into a crooked smile. 'Just as well for you that there are a couple of slices left.'

Amber watched the repartee between the two of them and relaxed. It seemed that Martyn was back to his old self, and Ethan was on top form. Maybe, if she gave it time, he would even let her within warming distance of his heart.

They went to Caitlin's house-warming party the next evening. Martyn was in jovial mood, enjoying the opportunity to mix with all the family and friends his daughter had invited.

There were distant uncles, aunts and cousins, and they all seemed intent on having a joyful get-together.

Amber kept a careful eye on Martyn to make sure he wasn't overdoing things, but he appeared to be coping well enough. Whenever she looked his way, he was chuckling at something someone was saying or admiring the gardens that Caitlin was trying to cultivate.

'He seems to be doing fine, doesn't he?' Ethan said, coming over to her and handing her a glass of rum punch.

'Yes. It's lovely to see him looking so cheerful.' She sipped her drink, enjoying the exotic flavour, and after a while she laid her glass down on a nearby table.

He slid an arm around her waist. 'Come and see the palm grove,' he murmured. 'Ben and Molly offered to keep an eye on Martyn for a while.'

He led her to the foot of a grassy hill some short distance from the house, where ferns grew in abundance and trees made majestic silhouettes against the skyline. Darkness was falling, and the air was heavy with the scent of tropical flowers. The faint clicking sound of a gecko could be heard in the distance. It was peaceful out here, away from the bustle of people and the background hum of gentle music.

'This must feel a little strange to you,' Ethan said, 'meeting our family, while yours is so far away. You said, a while back, how difficult it was getting used to being away from home.'

She nodded. 'I thought I would be all right, but I've never been away for such a long time before. Of course, I talk to my parents on the phone, and I see them over the video link, but it isn't quite the same. I think they've been arguing lately, but I can't get to the bottom of what's happening. They seem a bit tense with one another. I know my father's busy with the medical practice. My mother is still a bit out of synch with everything. She isn't usually rattled easily, but my coming here didn't sit well with her for some reason.'

'Will they come over here to visit, do you think?'

'I hope so.' She leaned back against the trunk of a palm tree and gazed around. 'They talked about coming here in a couple of months. I'm sure they'll love it as much as I do.'

'The romance of the island is finding its way into your heart. It happens to everyone after a while. It casts a spell on you, and you never want to leave.'

He came to stand in front of her, laying a hand on the bole of the tree just above her head, and then he leaned towards her, dropping a kiss lightly on her mouth. 'I hadn't expected it to happen,' he said softly, 'but you've made a huge impact on my life. You caught me unawares, and now I can't stop thinking about you, day or night.'

He gave a half-smile, his gaze running over her. 'Especially in the night.' He kissed her again, teasing the softness of her lips with the brush of his mouth, enticing a flurry of expectation within her nervous system, stoking the flame that burned inside her.

He ran his finger along the line of her throat and let it trail downwards, shifting over the full curve of her breast, until his hand came to rest beneath its ripe mound, cupping her gently.

Heat pooled in her abdomen, and Amber felt

her legs go weak. He moved closer, his long body lightly pressuring hers, his kisses filling her with sweet anticipation. She wanted this to go on and on. For this moment he was hers, and hers alone.

She wound her arms around his neck, loving the feel of him, her mouth softening beneath his. He kissed her face, her throat, and dipped lower to brush his lips over the creamy swell of her breasts.

Then the reality of the world intruded on them. The sound of voices erupted from the house some distance away, and the spell was broken in an instant. Ethan eased himself away from her as the noise increased, and chattering people spilled out onto the garden terrace. Amber straightened, moving away from the palm tree, looking towards Caitlin's new home.

'People are getting ready to leave,' Ethan murmured. 'I suppose we'd better go and find my uncle and round up Molly and Ben.'

She nodded. The tantalising, wonderful moment had gone almost has soon as it had occurred, and she felt an overpowering sense of loss. She loved Ethan. It came to her in a startling flare of revelation that threatened to overwhelm her with its forcefulness. Her life would never be the same again. She loved this man, and she realised now that she had never felt this way before. It was all-consuming, a love that she knew with certainty would stay with her for all the years to come.

And yet she couldn't help feeling that it was a revelation she could have done without. For Ethan had made no sign that he loved her in return. He wanted her, desired her, but that was not at all the same thing.

They walked back to the house and took their leave of Caitlin and James just a short time later. 'That was a good party,' Martyn told his daughter and her new husband. 'It's lovely to see you settled here. I just know you're going to be very happy.'

The journey home was a short one, and Amber left Martyn to chat with Ethan for a while. 'It was a great night,' she said, 'but I have to make an early start in the morning. I'll see you both tomorrow.'

Over the next few days, she tried to concentrate

on her work at the hospital. The rota meant that she was based in the Accident and Emergency unit this month, while another doctor went out on calls.

Ethan had been asked to go and help the bosses at his former hospital with planning arrangements to co-ordinate emergency services throughout the region. It meant that Amber saw very little of him during that time. He dropped in on Martyn every day, to see how he was doing, but mostly he worked late into the evenings and continued with his emergency call outs as usual.

'Mr Martyn has appointed extra people to take charge at the plantation,' Molly told Amber one day at breakfast. 'I think he was worried that Mr Ethan would find it too much to cope with, running the business, as well as working at the hospital.'

'Is Ethan all right with that?'

'Am I all right with what?' Ethan came into the dining room and helped himself to a buttered croissant along with apricot preserve. He sat down at the table, biting into the croissant and wiping crumbs from his mouth.

Amber watched him in fascination. How was

it that everything about him drew her attention and held her absorbed whenever he was around? 'Are you all right with having managers appointed to take over from you at the plantation?'

'I'm fine with it,' he said, taking another bite and pouring a cup of coffee. He lifted the pot and raised a questioning brow, indicating Amber's cup. She pushed it towards him and he gave her a refill. 'I asked him to make the changes,' he said, putting the coffeepot back on its stand, 'and I suggested the people I wanted to fill the slots.'

'Does that mean you're going back to your job at the main hospital?' Amber asked. She finished off her omelette and laid down her knife and fork, taking a sip of hot coffee.

He shook his head. 'We're setting up a new joint system, making it a smoother process to deal with emergencies. I'll probably be based at both hospitals. It should prove interesting.' He finished off his coffee and looked around. 'What's happened to Martyn this morning? Is he running late? He's usually joined us by now.'

'I looked in on him, but he said he was still

tired and said he would have a bit of a lie-in this morning,' Molly said. 'I told him I would take a breakfast tray up to him.' She indicated the tray she was preparing. The plate was covered to keep the food warm, and she was adding freshly squeezed orange juice along with croissants and preserve. 'I'll take this upstairs now and see if he's feeling more rested.'

Molly left the room and Amber glanced at Ethan across the table. He had just finished off his third croissant and was starting on a plate of scrambled eggs and ham.

'What?' he said. 'Something wrong?'

She hid a grin. 'Nothing at all. I've no idea where you put it.' There wasn't an ounce of fat to spare on him. He was long and lean, with muscles honed to perfection, and she guessed that was a result of him being constantly on the move, full of energy. He was bursting with vitality, always up for the next challenge.

'Hmm.' He looked her over, starting with the silky length of her hair, and moving down to linger on the smooth, bare flesh of her arms before gliding over the fullness of her curves. 'I'd say you had things just about right. No need for you to diet, obviously. That heavenly feminine shape is perfection itself.'

Warm colour flowed into her cheeks. He had caught her out in staring at him and paid her back in kind. Did he really like the way she looked? A little glow started up in her.

Molly came back into the room just then. 'Mr Ethan…' she said, and then she stopped.

'Yes, Molly, what is it?' He glanced towards the doorway where she stood, and for a second or two Molly simply stayed there, just looking at him and saying nothing.

It was clear that the housekeeper was upset, and both Ethan and Amber stood up to go over to her.

'Molly, what's wrong?' Ethan placed an arm around Molly's shoulders, looking down at her as though he would comfort her in any way he could.

'It's Mr Martyn. I don't know what to do. You should go up to him.'

Ethan nodded and sent a quick glance towards Amber to let her know that she should take care of Molly. Then he strode out of the room and went quickly upstairs.

'Come and sit down, Molly,' Amber urged, helping her into a seat. 'What's wrong with Martyn, do you know? Is he struggling for breath?'

Molly shook her head. 'I don't think he's breathing at all. I think he's gone, passed away. He was just lying there, so peaceful, and I thought he was sleeping, but he didn't wake when I spoke to him, and then I realised that he'd gone.'

Molly reached for a hanky from her pocket and began to wipe her eyes. 'He was such a lovely man.'

Amber stared at her in shock. She tried to comfort her, and all the while she was thinking that she should go to Martyn, but Ethan was with him and if what Molly had said was true, Ethan might want to be alone with his uncle for a while. If he'd needed help, he would have called her, wouldn't he?

She waited, desperately wanting to hear him shout her name so that she could go to help. That would mean that something could be done, wouldn't it?

But Ethan didn't call, and Amber stayed with Molly until Ben came to see what was happening and find out why Martyn hadn't arrived to go through the list of jobs for the day with him.

'Will you stay with Molly, Ben? I need to go and find out how Ethan is coping.'

Ben nodded, and turned to comfort his wife. Amber hurried out of the room and went in search of Ethan, stopping to knock quietly on the door of Martyn's room.

'Ethan, are you all right in there? Is there anything I can do to help?'

He didn't answer, and it was a while before she heard him walk across the room towards the door. 'There's nothing anyone can do,' he said. 'It's too late. It's over.'

She looked beyond him to where Martyn was lying on the bed. Like Molly had said, he seemed to be at peace, the remnants of a faint smile on his face, and she said huskily, 'I'm so sorry, Ethan.' Tears were trickling down her cheeks, but she let them fall. Martyn had been good to her and to everyone around him, and it was only fitting that his loss should be mourned.

Ethan didn't say very much at all over the next hour or so. It was as though he was in shock, and Amber reflected that they were all in much the same state.

Over the next few days she helped the family with the arrangements that had to be made, and she stood with them alongside Molly and Ben as Martyn was finally laid to rest in a secluded corner of the cemetery where his ancestors were buried.

She helped prepare a reception for family and friends who came to pay their respects, and she was amazed by the number of people who came to grieve for him. 'He was such a well-respected man,' his plantation manager said. 'His name will go on for years to come. Everyone who knew him will have something good to say about him.'

Ethan thanked everyone for coming to the house. 'Caitlin and I have been overwhelmed by your thoughtfulness and consideration,' he told the gathering. 'We've lost a truly great man, a man who did so much to provide work for people on the island, and who has been responsible for serving a community way beyond these shores. I know he would want to thank you for the help you gave him over the years, and he would value the work you do in keeping on with the traditions he set in place.'

Amber walked around as though she was in a daze. She mingled with people in the house, and spoke to visitors who assembled outside on the terrace. She comforted Caitlin as best she could, and through it all she wanted to wrap her arms around Ethan and hold him close.

He was distant from her, though, wrapped up in his own grief. He was finding it difficult to relate to anyone at all just then, and Amber realised that all she could do was let him know that she was here for him if he needed her.

After a few days Amber went back to work and made an effort to adjust to life without Martyn's presence. He had promised her the use of the bungalow for as long as she needed it, and Ethan had continued to expect her to join them up at the house as before. She didn't know how much longer things would go on this way, though. Now that Martyn had gone, her position in the household was precarious and she was uncertain as to how she should go on.

'The family solicitor is coming over to the house late this afternoon,' Ethan told her one morning as she was preparing to leave for work. 'He wants everyone to meet up for the reading of my uncle's will. Given the intricacies of the estate, it might go on for a couple of hours, so Molly's going to prepare coffee and snacks. We should have enough room for everyone to be seated in the main reception room.'

'Okay,' she said. 'Thanks for telling me. I'll keep out of the way. I have plenty of chores to keep me busy back at the bungalow.'

'No,' he said. 'Leave them for another time, please. The solicitor says you're mentioned in the will, so you should be there.'

Amber stared at him. 'Why would Martyn have left me anything? And how is that possible? He didn't say anything about changing his will, did he?'

'No, he didn't. But, then, he invited the lawyers over to the house a few weeks ago, and he was fairly offhand about his reasons, wasn't he?' He sent her a brief, assessing look. 'I knew something had to be going on with him. It was odd, him bringing you over here in the first place...generous and altruistic maybe, but I always felt there was something more to it than that.'

Amber breathed in deeply. She had no idea what had been going on in Martyn's mind, but it was obvious that Ethan still had doubts as to his motives. She could only hope that the reading of the will would make everything clear, and that the uncertainty could be cleared up once and for all.

CHAPTER TEN

'Now we come to the main bequests,' the solicitor said, addressing the people who were gathered together in the reception room. He had been talking for over an hour already, dealing mainly with issues concerning the continued running of the plantation, the various overseas assets and the gifts and legacies that Martyn had bequeathed to distant family members. Molly and Ben had each inherited a good-sized sum of money and one of the bungalows on the estate. Amber's name had not been mentioned so far, and she was beginning to wonder if Ethan had made a mistake when he had asked her to be there.

Perhaps he simply wanted her to support him through this final ordeal. Hearing Martyn's wishes laid out this way had been difficult, because it was as though he was still speaking to them, letting them know how much he cherished each and every one of them.

Ethan learned that he was to inherit a large chunk of the business, along with a sizeable fortune and the house that they were sitting in at this moment. It meant that he was the main shareholder, owning around sixty-five per cent of the whole.

Amber was startled by that information. Why would Martyn have left Ethan the house? Shouldn't it have gone to Caitlin? Perhaps it was because of the land that went with it…as a member of the Brookes family, and half-owner of the plantation, maybe it was his true inheritance.

Caitlin was to have another portion of the business, amounting to some seventeen and a half per cent. She, too, was given a sizeable fortune, and her trust fund was to be opened up so that she would have an amount to live on each year. There were also various properties left to her.

'Last, but not least, Mr Wyndham Brookes has made provision for Amber Shaw,' the solicitor said. 'Miss Shaw, for you there is the remaining seventeen and a half per cent of the business, and the bungalow in which you are living at present. There is also a sum of money.'

Amber was already struggling to take in what the solicitor was saying. When he mentioned the amount of money that was to be hers, the colour drained from her face and she thought that she was going to faint. She sucked in a shaky breath. Surely the solicitor had it all wrong? It was someone else who had inherited this fortune, not her.

Caitlin had gasped as the last part of the will was being read out. Amber saw the shock on her face, and when she looked towards Ethan, she saw that he, too, was stunned. His jaw was set in a rigid line, as though he couldn't quite take it in.

The solicitor was still speaking. 'There is a letter for you, Dr Shaw. Mr Wyndham Brookes suggested that you might want to read it in private.'

'There has to be some mistake,' Amber said. 'Why would Martyn leave me anything at all? Perhaps there's been a mix-up over the name?'

He shook his head and gave a brief smile.

'There is no mistake. I believe you will find that everything is explained in the letter.'

The solicitor looked towards Caitlin and Ethan. 'There are letters for both of you, as well. Mr Wyndham Brookes felt that you should know something of the reasoning behind these legacies.'

Amber was shaking as she accepted the envelope from the solicitor. All about her the meeting was breaking up as people went to help themselves to more coffee or stood about in small groups, talking to one another.

'If there is anything you want to ask, or you need any help at all, please get in touch with me,' the solicitor said. He handed her an embossed card. 'My number… You can reach me during office hours with that, but my mobile number is on the card, as well, in case you have a problem at any other time.'

'Thank you.'

She got to her feet and straightened up. Caitlin was wearing a bemused expression, and Amber felt she needed to go over to her. She had to let her know that she had no idea what Martyn had intended.

'Caitlin, this has all come as a huge shock to me. I didn't know this was in his mind. I can't explain it.'

Caitlin nodded. 'I'm not really concerned about the inheritance, or the money side of things but, as you say, it has come as a shock to all of us.'

Amber looked at Ethan. 'Perhaps you should read this letter with me. I've nothing to hide. I can't begin to imagine what it says.'

He shook his head. 'He said it would be best if you went somewhere to read it in private. You should do that, and maybe we can talk later. We've all had a lot to take in this afternoon.' He glanced at Caitlin. 'Are you all right? I know this has been difficult for you.'

Caitlin gave him a watery smile. 'I think I need to go and walk outside for a while with James. I feel as though my father's presence is all around, and I still can't get used to the fact that he isn't coming back.'

Ethan nodded, and watched her leave the room with James at her side. He turned back to Amber. 'I have to go and talk to the rest of the family.

Perhaps you and I could meet up in an hour or so and talk things through?'

'Yes, that sounds like a good idea. I'll go back to the bungalow. Like Caitlin said, it's all a bit overwhelming here right now.'

She left the house and walked along the path to the bungalow. It was inconceivable that Martyn would have left it to her. What had he been thinking?

She went into her sitting-room and sat down on the sofa, staring down at the envelope that was still clutched in her fingers. Would the letter tell her everything she wanted to know? What had been going through Martyn's mind when he'd made that extraordinary bequest?

She carefully tore open the envelope and drew out the sheet of paper inside. Martyn's bold, black handwriting filled the page.

My dear Amber, you're probably very puzzled right now, and wondering what this inheritance is all about.

I'll try to explain. The truth of the matter

goes back many years, to when I lived in London and our offices were near what is now the Docklands area. We needed the services of an advertising company, and your mother came along to do a presentation for us. I was completely knocked out by her. She was stunning, and I fell for her, hook, line and sinker. We had only known each other for a short time when I was called back to Hawaii to take over the running of the plantation. I wanted your mother to come with me, but she wasn't ready to take that step.

Anyway, we parted company, and I missed her. I wrote to her for a while, but then it became obvious that the distance between us was a huge barrier, and the letters petered out.

I didn't have any more communication with her until after you and I met just a few months ago. I was very curious as to what had happened to her in the intervening years. In retrospect, I'm pleased that she married soon after I left for Hawaii all those years ago. I trust she's had a happy marriage, and she must surely be proud that she has produced such a beautiful, intelligent and caring daughter.

I think it best if I leave it to your mother to explain the rest to you. Take this legacy I have given you and enjoy it. I'm so pleased to have met you, and come to know you, even though it has been for such a short time.

If you need help with anything in the future, you should look to Ethan. He has been like a son to me, and I know he is the one you should turn to for whatever you might need.

Take care of yourself, and have a happy future.

Martyn

Amber read the letter over and over again. He had said so much, and yet so little. Why was he leaving it to her mother to tell her the rest? What more was there to tell?

She began to pace the room. It was astonishing to learn that he and her mother had fallen for one another all those years ago. But perhaps her mother had not had quite the same depth of feeling for Martyn, or maybe the thought of leaving home and travelling halfway across the world with him had been too much for her.

There was a soft tapping at her door, and Amber pulled herself together and went to answer it.

Ethan stood there, looking at her guardedly, and she knew he must wonder what her letter contained.

'Come into the sitting-room,' she said. 'I've opened the glass doors to let the ocean breeze into the house. It's beautiful at this time of the day as the sun's going down. I love looking out over the water.'

His gaze travelled over her. 'Are you going to tell me what my uncle had to say? You don't have to, of course, if you'd rather keep it private.'

'Didn't he explain things in his letter to you?'

He shook his head. 'He simply said that he wanted us to treat you as part of the family. He asked Caitlin to think of you as a sister. For my part, he offered advice as to the best course of action for the future.'

She frowned. 'What would that be?'

He gave a rueful smile. 'Perhaps we should find out what's actually going on here before we start looking into that. Are you going to tell me what he said, or is it something you need to keep secret?'

'It isn't a secret…but it isn't anything I really understand, either.' She handed him the letter.

He read it carefully, and then looked up, frowning as he studied her features. 'He told me that you look very much like your mother did when she was your age,' he said in a quiet voice.

'Yes. That's true, and maybe I reminded him of her. But why has he left so much to be guessed at? Why does he want me to talk to my mother about it?'

'You don't know?'

She gave a shuddery sigh. 'I can guess…but the answer turns my world upside down, and I can't believe that it could be true. Why hasn't he said what he means in the letter?'

Ethan's mouth made a wry shape. 'I'd say that was typical of my uncle. He doesn't want anyone to be hurt and so he's leaving it to the one person who has most to lose to tell you the truth. That way it's up to her as to how much anyone needs to know.'

Amber pressed her lips together. 'So you think I'm actually his daughter? Where does that leave my father…the man I've always called my father? I don't believe he has any idea about this, or surely he would have said something?'

She stared at Ethan, her eyes filling with tears. 'What am I supposed to do? How can this possibly be true?'

Ethan handed her the phone. 'There's only one way to find out,' he said. 'Talk to your mother.'

She stared at the phone. Everything she had ever believed had been turned on its head. In just a few short hours the world, as she knew it, had changed. If her mother confirmed what Martyn had been hinting at, then she was truly his daughter. It meant that Caitlin was her half-sister. And Ethan, what did it mean for her and Ethan? Was Ethan her cousin?

A wave of nausea swamped her. She handed the phone back to him. 'No, I can't. I don't want to know,' she said. 'I can't handle this. Everything was going along reasonably well, and now it's all gone wrong. It's chaos. I don't know who I am any more.' She paced the room once more. 'Besides, it must be early morning back home. I can't ring, out of the blue, and disturb everyone.'

'I expect it will be breakfast-time,' he said, thrusting the phone back into her hand once more. 'Didn't you tell me your father leaves early for the surgery? It's possible that your mother will be alone right now. This is probably the best time of all for you to call her.' He looked at her. 'You can do this, Amber. Deal with it now and find out the truth, otherwise you'll be forever afraid of what you might find out.'

She could see the sense in what he was saying. Could she live her life not knowing if she and Ethan were related? This was something she had to clarify, no matter how painful the answers might be.

She dialled the number, and when her mother answered, she walked into the kitchen and sat down at the table. She didn't know whether Ethan followed her. All she knew was that making this phone call was one of the hardest things she'd ever had to do in her life.

'Oh, Amber, I knew this would happen as soon as you told me he had passed away. I've been dreading this moment.'

'So, is it true…what he's hinting at? Am I really his daughter?'

Her mother's voice broke. 'Yes, it's true.' She gave a heavy, shaky sigh. 'I should have said something before this. He called me and said he had spoken to the lawyers. I knew then I had to say something.'

'But you didn't. Why didn't you tell me from the first?' Amber was struggling to come to terms with what was happening. How could her mother have deceived her for so long?

'I was afraid this would happen…that it would all come out,' her mother said. There was a catch in her voice, and a soft note of resignation threaded through her words. 'It was all such a long time ago now. He swept me off my feet, and

I couldn't think straight back then. He was like a whirlwind that blew through my life.'

'But you must have let him go without telling him that you were pregnant.' Amber frowned. 'How could you do that?'

'I didn't know I was pregnant until after Martyn left the country. And then, when I found out, I was so scared. You need to understand that my parents were very strict, and they would never have understood or condoned a pregnancy outside marriage. By then, though, I'd already met your father. I had a job to do in Henley-on-Thames, and your father was working there. We fell in love, and he asked me to marry him.'

She hesitated. 'He didn't know about the baby…or about Martyn. I told him I'd been involved with someone before he came along, but that was all. I said it was over between me and this other man, and I wanted to tell him about the baby, but I was afraid that he wouldn't understand. His parents were much the same as mine. They'd have thought very badly of me if they had realised the truth.'

'Don't you think my father would have guessed?'

Her mother sighed. 'We were very young, and innocent, despite what you might think. I kept quiet and let everyone think that you were born prematurely…even your father. You were tiny, and he didn't seem to suspect the truth. I felt really bad about deceiving him, but he loved you so much, and I couldn't bear to hurt him by telling him how things really were. As time went on, it was harder than ever to let him know what had really happened. We couldn't have any other children and I didn't want to hurt him by telling him that you weren't his. And I couldn't risk your grandparents knowing that I'd made a mistake. They would have thought so badly of me, and I didn't want them to treat you differently because of what I'd done.'

'Surely they wouldn't have?' Amber was finding her mother's confession difficult to absorb. Then her mother made a small hiccuping sound, and Amber wondered if she was crying. 'Mum…you have to know, I don't blame you for any of this,' she said. 'I just needed to know the truth, that's all. This has all come as such a shock.'

'I know. I'm sorry, Amber. I'm sorry I deceived everyone. I knew it couldn't go on, but I didn't know how to put it right without destroying everything.'

'What will you do?' Amber sucked in a long breath. 'I don't want you or Dad to feel badly about this…but he'll want to know why I have this inheritance, won't he? What will you tell him?'

Her mother gave a shuddery sigh. 'I've already spoken to him about it. After Martyn rang to tell me about the changes to his will, I realised I had to tell your father the truth. I should have done it a long time ago.'

'How did he take it?'

'Not very well. I'm still not sure that he's come to terms with it. And then I knew I had to tell you, but I didn't want to do it from such a distance. I thought maybe I could wait until you came home, or until we went out there to see you.'

Amber could see now why her mother had

been so unsettled by her meeting with Martyn and her decision to come out to Hawaii. It had set off a chain of events that would have repercussions for a long while to come.

They spoke for a while longer and then Amber ended the call and sat for a while, thinking things over. She turned to see that Ethan was standing in the kitchen, watching her closely.

'You heard?' she asked, and he nodded.

'Shall we go for a walk along the beach?' he suggested. 'I think you need time to absorb all this. It's been a momentous day for you, hasn't it?'

She looked at him, then stood up and placed her hands palms flat against his chest. 'Ethan, I think I should leave this place and go away somewhere. Somewhere far away. I don't think I can stay here and live life the same way as we have been doing these last few months. I have a half-sister I didn't know about, and getting used to that will take me some time, but I don't think I'll ever come to terms with the fact that you and I are cousins.'

She felt very close to tears. 'That's something I can't cope with right now. I need to put some distance between us. I'm sorry. I'm too close to you and it's all wrong. I've fallen in love with you over these last few months and it isn't right. I wish none of this had ever happened.' She tried to move away from him, but Ethan put his arm around her and pulled her close to him.

'You're wrong,' he said. 'We're not cousins at all. In theory, maybe we are, but Martyn was never a blood relative. His father was John Wyndham, and when his parents' marriage broke up, his mother married into the Brookes family. There were no children from that second marriage, and so there are no blood ties. He's my uncle because he was brought up alongside my father. You don't need to worry on that account.'

'I don't?' She stared up at him, scarcely able to believe what he was saying.

'You don't.' He kept his arm around her. 'Let's go and walk along the beach and see if we can find an answer to all this, shall we? I don't want you to go away from here. I want you to stay by my side and let me show you how good life can be. I don't even want to contemplate life without you.'

'Are you sure about that?' They walked out of the house, arm in arm, and wandered down the footpath towards the beach. The sun was sinking beneath the horizon, leaving its fading red light to glow softly in the sky, and all was calm, the serene tropical night like balm to Amber's soul.

'I'm sure,' he said, as they started to walk along the beach. 'I never knew what it was that Martyn was hiding from me, but now I know that he had the best of reasons for keeping quiet. He didn't want to upset your mother's apple cart. He was leaving it to you to find the truth, and to her to decide whether or not she should tell your father.'

He let his hand rest against the small of her back. 'I'm glad this has all come out into the open. All I want now is to let you know how I feel about you. Martyn knew all along, and he gave me his blessing in his letter to me. I love you, Amber. *Aloha au ia'oe.*'

She stood very still and looked up at him. The sand was soft beneath her feet, and overhead the palm leaves danced in the faint breeze. 'I love you, Ethan. *Mau loa*. For ever.'

He lowered his head and kissed her tenderly, holding her close as though he would never let her go. She stayed locked in his embrace for a long, long time. So much had happened, she had learned so many things, but most of all she had learned that she loved Ethan with all her heart.

'He really gave us his blessing?' she asked softly, after a while.

Ethan smiled. 'He said I should put a ring on your finger before some other likely candidate came along and whipped you away from me.'

'That sounds like Martyn.'

'Yes.' Then he frowned. 'What's that noise?' Ethan moved back from her a little, trying to discern what was happening.

Amber could hear a light chirruping sound, and it took a moment before she realised that it was her mobile phone.

She glanced at the display. 'It's my mother,' she said, looking anxiously at Ethan. 'I hope she's all right. I feel as though I messed things up for her.'

He lightly squeezed her shoulder. 'You did what you thought was best. Answer it.'

'Hello, Mum.'

'No, Amber. It's your father.'

'Oh, Dad, I'm so glad to hear your voice. Are you all right? I thought you were usually at the surgery at this time?'

'Well, I was out on call, and I just dropped in home for a while. I could see that your mother was upset.'

'Was she?' Amber was cautious, not knowing what to say. She didn't want to cause her mother any more problems. She frowned and Ethan drew her nearer to him in a gesture of support.

'You know, she told me everything. About Martyn and all that happened. I just wanted you to know, Amber, that it's all right. I was hurt and angry to begin with, but it was more to do with the fact that your mother hadn't told me from the beginning. All along I had a feeling that things weren't quite right, but I loved you and accepted you as my own. The fact is, I love your mother, and I'm glad that she's told me everything now.

I just hope that you're okay with it. It must have come as a bolt from the blue.'

'Something like that,' she said. 'But, yes, I think I'm all right with it. It's a lot to take in. I just want you to know that to me you'll always be my dad. You've always been there for me, and that's what really matters. I love you both. Tell Mum for me, will you?'

'I will, Amber. She's here with me, and I'm sure she knows already.'

They cut the call after a while, and Amber turned to look up at Ethan once more. 'I think it's going to be all right,' she said. 'I don't know how they could have kept up the pretence for so long, each one worried about what the other would think.'

'Love does strange things to people,' Ethan murmured. 'It makes you blind, it drives you crazy, it causes you to do all sorts of things to protect yourself from being hurt.'

'Is that what happened to you?' She ran her fingers gently down his cheek.

'In a way. I knew that you were everything I

ever wanted, but I was afraid you would leave me high and dry. I tried to tell myself that you weren't for real and you would be heading back home just as soon as you tired of being out here. But you unlocked my heart and crept inside, and now I can't ever let you go.'

She smiled up at him. 'I'm not going anywhere,' she said huskily. She wrapped her arms around him and drew his head down towards hers, kissing him softly, her lips clinging, her body arching against him.

He sucked in a taut breath. 'If you're going to do that, we had better start making plans,' he said in a ragged voice.

'Plans?'

'For our wedding day,' he said. 'I wouldn't want history to repeat itself after all. You're taking me way too close to heaven, and I'm just a mere man. I don't have the willpower to resist you.'

She laughed softly. 'My parents are supposed to be coming over here soon, aren't they? Why don't we arrange it so they're coming for a very special celebration?'

'My thoughts exactly,' he said in a roughened tone. *'Nau ko'u aloha,'* he whispered. 'My love is yours. *Mau loa.* For ever.'

'For ever,' she echoed, and gave herself up to his kisses. The sun had gone down over the horizon, the night was young, and moonlight bathed them in its silvery glow. All was well with the world.

MEDICAL™

Large Print

Titles for the next six months…

January

DARE SHE DATE THE DREAMY DOC?	Sarah Morgan
DR DROP-DEAD GORGEOUS	Emily Forbes
HER BROODING ITALIAN SURGEON	Fiona Lowe
A FATHER FOR BABY ROSE	Margaret Barker
NEUROSURGEON…AND MUM!	Kate Hardy
WEDDING IN DARLING DOWNS	Leah Martyn

February

WISHING FOR A MIRACLE	Alison Roberts
THE MARRY-ME WISH	Alison Roberts
PRINCE CHARMING OF HARLEY STREET	Anne Fraser
THE HEART DOCTOR AND THE BABY	Lynne Marshall
THE SECRET DOCTOR	Joanna Neil
THE DOCTOR'S DOUBLE TROUBLE	Lucy Clark

March

DATING THE MILLIONAIRE DOCTOR	Marion Lennox
ALESSANDRO AND THE CHEERY NANNY	Amy Andrews
VALENTINO'S PREGNANCY BOMBSHELL	Amy Andrews
A KNIGHT FOR NURSE HART	Laura Iding
A NURSE TO TAME THE PLAYBOY	Maggie Kingsley
VILLAGE MIDWIFE, BLUSHING BRIDE	Gill Sanderson

MILLS & BOON®

MEDICAL™

Large Print

April

BACHELOR OF THE BABY WARD	Meredith Webber
FAIRYTALE ON THE CHILDREN'S WARD	Meredith Webber
PLAYBOY UNDER THE MISTLETOE	Joanna Neil
OFFICER, SURGEON…GENTLEMAN!	Janice Lynn
MIDWIFE IN THE FAMILY WAY	Fiona McArthur
THEIR MARRIAGE MIRACLE	Sue MacKay

May

DR ZINETTI'S SNOWKISSED BRIDE	Sarah Morgan
THE CHRISTMAS BABY BUMP	Lynne Marshall
CHRISTMAS IN BLUEBELL COVE	Abigail Gordon
THE VILLAGE NURSE'S HAPPY-EVER-AFTER	Abigail Gordon
THE MOST MAGICAL GIFT OF ALL	Fiona Lowe
CHRISTMAS MIRACLE: A FAMILY	Dianne Drake

June

ST PIRAN'S: THE WEDDING OF THE YEAR	Caroline Anderson
ST PIRAN'S: RESCUING PREGNANT CINDERELLA	Carol Marinelli
A CHRISTMAS KNIGHT	Kate Hardy
THE NURSE WHO SAVED CHRISTMAS	Janice Lynn
THE MIDWIFE'S CHRISTMAS MIRACLE	Jennifer Taylor
THE DOCTOR'S SOCIETY SWEETHEART	Lucy Clark

MILLS & BOON®